12⁵⁰

*To Mary Wright*
*Thank you for your*
*kind words, All best*
*Stephen March*

# Love
# to the
# Spirits

stories

by
## STEPHEN MARCH

RIVER CITY PUBLISHING
MONTGOMERY, ALABAMA

Published in the United States by River City Publishing
1719 Mulberry St.
Montgomery, AL 36106.

Designed by Lissa Monroe

First Edition—2004
Printed in the United States of America
     1 3 5 7 9 10 8 6 4 2

March, Stephen, 1948-
  Love to the spirits and other stories / by Stephen March.-- 1st ed.
     p. cm.
  ISBN 1-57966-057-6
  1. United States--Social life and customs--Fiction. I. Title.
  PS3613.A733L688 2004
  813'.6--dc22
                              2004009903

For Dino Nichols, 1956-1991
in memoriam

# Contents

# Acknowledgments

Thanks to the following publications, in which these stories were published.

"Sharks" appeared in *New Orleans Review*, "*A Good Gravedigger*" in *Tampa Review*, "*Love To The Spirits*" in the *William and Mary Review*, "Tusks" in *Appalachian Heritage*, "Starlene's Baby" in *Portland Review*, "The Driver" in the *Seattle Review*, "Disappearances" and "Angles" in *Carolina Quarterly*, "Adrift" in *Cold Mountain Review*, "Prowlers" in *Carolina Alumni Review* (as "Wisteria"), "Violets" in *Rio Grande Review*, and "Specks of Gold" in the *Crescent Review*.

Special thanks to Fred Chappell, Robert Donnan, Ashley Gordon, Mary March, and John Rosenthal.

# Sharks

My grandpa Roy and me are on a two-lane way out in West Texas, with nothing but cactus and sagebrush as far as the eye can see. I'm trying out new names for myself, since Roy recently reminded me we are going to have to change our names. Jenna Steel, Jenna Du Page, Jenna Royale. I consider changing my first name, too. "Evangeline," I whisper. That's a pretty name. I like Candace, too. Candace Troy. I want to ask Roy what he thinks about it, but he is talking about cabbages again.

"A cabbage is a good, simple vegetable," he says. "Nothing flashy about it. It's just what it is, all leaves and heart. Did you know eating cabbages can keep you from getting cancer?"

I tell him I have to use the bathroom, and he says there is a town up ahead. Where could a town hide in country like this? All I can see are miles and miles of sun-baked ground.

But there is a town. Comes up out of nowhere. Steam hissing from under the hood, the truck clanks and wheezes into a Texaco station just past a sign, "Delphia, pop. 5,150." While Roy talks to a mechanic I visit the john. Then my dog Cody and me walk around back to stretch our legs. Shell casings and oil cans litter the cracked, dusty ground. A cactus, shot full of holes, leans crazily to the side. The sinking sun paints everything copper.

I sit on a cinder block and imagine meeting my True Love after we get to California. A tall, slim boy with dark brown hair and eyes. I picture him touching my face, gazing into my eyes with adoration. *Candace, I'm so glad I found you* . . .

Cody's bark snaps me out of my daydream. He is moving backwards, like a film run in reverse. Nearby a snake is coiled up and ready to strike, its forked tongue stabbing the air.

"Cody!" I scoop him up in my arms and go look for Roy.

9

I find him standing by the truck, talking to a man with yellow stains under his armpits. The truck's hood is up.

"Engine could be shot," the man says. "Then again your water pump might be froze up. We can look at it in the morning."

Roy looks disgusted. "Ready to spend another night in the truck, Jenna?"

"I guess so." I can see now isn't the time to mention Roy promised me a motel room tonight. What the heck, I think, things could be worse. Could have been snake-bit.

I listen to the gas station man give Roy directions to the nearest pool hall. "Go on into town. Turn left at the second light. You'll see Mom's Billiards on the left about halfway down the block."

While Roy pulls the truck around to the side of the station, I feed and water Cody. I tie him to the rear bumper with a rope. Roy gets his Panama hat out of the cab, then locks everything up. We walk into town, stopping at a 7-Eleven for hot dogs, fries, and drinks. The hot dogs are smothered in chili and onions. I am hungry enough to eat three of them, but I only eat two because I know it can affect my game if I eat too much.

Pieces of chili cling to Roy's beard. It's frosty white, like what little hair he has left on his head. He says his hair was tar-black when he was young. Claims he was six-one then, too, although he can't be more than five-ten now, max. Where'd those inches go? I asked him once. He said, "Gravity."

Roy is my daddy's daddy. We are on our way to Fresno, California, where Roy owns a one-third interest in a farm. He inherited his share of the farm from an uncle a few years back, and Roy's half brother and a cousin have been managing it since then. The farm has strawberries and cantaloupes growing on it, but the big money crop is cabbage. Roy likes the idea of making money off cabbages. He is looking forward to sitting in a rocking chair and watching them grow. Farm life will be good for me, too, he says, pointing out that I'll get lots of fresh air, exercise, and good food. He says I'll have to buckle down at school and do all my homework before I can even touch a pool stick.

10

We left Virginia in a hurry, intending to head straight across country, but after we got on the road Roy decided we should go to Florida first, then work our way west, hitting the pool halls along the way. This was so we could put together a stake for my college education. I don't know how much money we've made, but it's a pile. Roy is the coach, and I'm the hands and eyes.

Before he got cataracts and "the old age shakes" in his hands, Roy was one of the best hustlers on the East Coast. He knew and played the legends — guys like Rudolph "Minnesota Fats" Wanderone, Willie Mosconi, Wimpy Lassiter, and Arthur Kelly. Roy says the best players never went penguin and played in tournaments. They just used their skill to make a living as sharks. He says he won a fortune at pool and spent most of it on "good times and fast living."

I was seven when Roy came to live with us. That was five years ago, a few months after my mom had left my daddy and me for her boss, Dr. Bob Conari. Roy cooked, kept the house clean, and looked after me when my daddy was at work. Daddy, who didn't see Roy much when he was growing up, said Roy made a better mom than my mother, Fay. Since my daddy worked sixty- and seventy-hour weeks at his used car lot, I spent most of my time with Roy. We played pool every day on the table in the den. In fact, that's about all we did. When my daddy was there we'd play cutthroat. After I got good, Roy taught me to work a hustle. How to play below my true speed and how to dump a stroke and lemon to keep the sucker in the game. I practiced on the players at McDuffy's Billiards with Roy coaching, but it wasn't long before I became a face, and I couldn't get much action.

Roy said I was a natural, with a better eye and more talent than anyone he'd ever seen, which sure made my head swell. That's about the nicest thing anyone ever said to me.

My happy life ended after my daddy killed his business partner, Rupert Charles. My daddy says it was an accident. They had a falling out over money, and when Rupert went for the pistol he kept in his desk drawer, Daddy grabbed it and it went off. Which sounds believable to me, considering what I know about Rupert. He used to roll back the mileage on cars until my daddy made him stop, and he'd pinch me on the bottom when no one was looking. The two big holes in my daddy's story are that Rupert was shot three times and him and my daddy were both dating the same woman.

Jury didn't believe my daddy. Last time I saw him he was sitting behind a Plexiglas window in the state penitentiary. He looked awful—pale and skinny, dark circles under his eyes. "Are you being a good girl, Jenna?" he asked "Are you staying away from bad influences?"

After my daddy got arrested, I wanted to go on living with Roy, but a judge sent me to live with my mom, who wouldn't let me play pool. "That's a game for lowlifes," she said. "You need to take up something like ballet or the piano." She made me leave my custom stick with Roy.

I like my daddy a lot better than Fay, whose perfume makes me sneeze and whose idea of a good time is going shopping. She has about a million pairs of shoes and more dresses than the queen of England. Her new husband is a stomach doctor with a big, pink face that reminds me of an orchid I once saw growing in a hothouse.

Although I wasn't crazy about the arrangement, I honestly tried to make it work with my mom and Bob Conari—until the night he came into my room and wanted me to do something nasty. When I told my mother about this, she accused me of trying to break up her marriage.

"Bob Conari is the best thing that ever happened to me, and I'm not about to let my present happiness be tainted by your hateful lies," she said. "Your problem is you take after certain trashy elements on your daddy's side of the family. If you don't straighten up I'm gonna send you to Social Services. Know where you'll end up? In a foster home. You might even get placed with a Negro family, and wouldn't that be something?"

A few nights later, I woke up with Bob Conari in my bed, buck naked and breathing whiskey fumes in my face. "It won't do you any good to make a fuss," he said. "Fay's had enough gin to knock down a horse." Wasn't any way I could fight him off. He weighs over two hundred and I only weigh eighty-eight. "I'll do what you want," I told him, "only I need to use the bathroom first." He let me go then, telling me to hurry it up, but I locked the bathroom door and wouldn't come out. I told him to go away, that I was feeling sick on my stomach. He pounded on the door so hard I thought he was going to break it down before he finally gave up and slithered off to bed.

I spent the rest of the night in there.

Next morning after Bob left for his office, I stole all the money out of my mom's pocketbook. Instead of catching the bus to school I took off through the woods with Cody, a little brown mutt my daddy brought home one day, and walked the two miles to Daddy's house.

Roy was sitting in the front yard, holding a bottle of beer in one hand, a fly swatter in the other. He wanted to know why I wasn't in school. When I told him what my mom's sorry excuse for a husband had done, Roy flew hot. He went into the house and began looking for his pistol. "Please don't shoot him, Roy," I begged. "If you do that, they'll put you in jail, too, and then who'll I have left?"

I cried and carried on so much Roy put his gun away. He admitted I had made a couple of good points and that maybe he ought to think things through first. To unwind, we played a little rotation, after which he got the idea of us going to California to live on his cabbage farm. He said he would call Daddy and explain the situation to him.

"What if they track us down?" I asked.

Roy said we could change our names and no one would find us.

"America is a big country. People disappear all the time here and are never heard from again."

"What happens to them?"

"Some create a whole new life for themselves," Roy said, stroking his beard. "Others just vanish into the atmosphere."

I wasn't sure what Roy meant about people vanishing, but I liked the idea of us starting over in California, since it's on the other side of the country from Dr. Bob Conari. From listening to Roy I pictured California as a place with land so rich and fertile I could throw some seeds out the back door and a few months later there would be an orchard of fruit trees growing there, with delicious apples and oranges all ripe in the sun.

Down the street from the pool hall, Roy takes out his one-ounce bottle of whiskey. He pours some in his hands, rubs it into his beard, then we go in. There's a counter to the right, and sitting behind it is the fattest woman I have ever seen. She is so big she looks like she has been blown up with air. Fat hangs from her jaws in jiggly rolls.

We'd like to rent a table," Roy says.

"Three bucks an hour. Mom keeps time."

"You must be Mom."

"That's right. You got a gun, give it to me and pick it up when you leave."

Roy pats his pockets. "Ain't packing nothing, ma'am, 'cept a heart full of good intentions."

"I can see that all right. No foul language and no minors."

"My granddaughter is sixteen."

"Sure she is."

Roy puts twelve dollars on the counter. "Looks like you run a clean place."

"Find a roach here and I'll eat it," Mom says.

"I believe it." Roy tips his hat to her, and we walk back to the tables. There are about a dozen tables in the low-ceilinged room, half of them in use. Each table lit by a bare bulb suspended from the ceiling. Spectators' benches line the walls.

We select sticks from the rack and get a table at the back so Roy can have a hawk's view of the room and other players. My stick isn't bad for an off-the-rack, but I miss the good hitter Roy gave me for Christmas. It stays in the truck since a two-piece custom cue would blow our setup. We shoot a game of 9-ball. While Roy is busy sharking a mark, I try to get a feel for the table. The locals have the edge here because they are usually familiar with every bump and dimple. They know how hard to hit a shot, how much bounce is in the rail, which pocket is tight, which one is a sewer, which ball rolls crooked due to its flecks and nicks.

I could stay here all night learning this doozy. The green is dusty as a cowboy's hat, which slows down the ivories.

It doesn't take Roy long to peg everyone in the room. The top stick, the wannabes, the bangers, the fish, the squares. He lays a twenty on the side rail, and I see him nod to this guy across the room.

The man sashays over to our table. He is wearing snakeskin boots and a Stetson with a red feather stuck in the band. He has long arms and legs, a potbelly, and ice-blue eyes with no lashes to speak of. His pale skin and pearl-handled stick say he's a serious player. (Roy and me sit out in the sun every day to stay tan.)

They shoot a lag for the break, and Roy wins by half an inch. I sit on the bench and watch them play. Red Feather keeps the first couple of games close enough to be interesting but lemons off the 9-ball. Not a bad dump stroke, I think. He seems smoother than most of the resident studs I play. They're usually all flash, with no interest in playing a good defense. They bank on their skill at sinking rocks instead of considering the layout after they shoot.

Red Feather's acting isn't bad, either.

"That shot was dead center," he says, after a stall that locks up a game for Roy. "Green has got more bumps than a toad."

He has nasty personal habits, like picking at his rump, belching, digging around in his crotch with his long, hairy fingers. When I play him, I'll need to tune out these distractions.

After each game Roy swills from his flask, which contains only prune juice. The more he loses, the madder he acts. "Damn these lights in here," he says. "What kind of bulbs they got up there—twenty-watt?"

Watching him lose, I roll my eyes, glare, groan, and pout. A couple of the cowboys on the benches give me sympathetic looks, but no one says anything. No knockers here. Oh, Jenna, I think. You should be in the movies.

Reeling the sucker in, Roy loses about three hundred before he sits on the bench, his head in his hands. "My eyes just ain't as good as they used to be."

I put my hand on his shoulder. "Grandpa, let's go now."

Red Feather looks at us like we are something squishy he just stepped in on the sidewalk. "Had enough, huh?"

"Nosiree Bob!" Roy says. "You think you're really good, but I'll bet my granddaughter here can beat you."

"Grandpa, stop it and let's go!"

Red Feather sneers, shakes his head.

Roy pulls out a roll of bills. "A G-note says she can beat your ass."

"You want me to play this kid?"

Roy lays a thousand-dollar bill on the side rail.

"A grand says she can beat you, five ahead."

"You got yourself a bet, old timer."

"Grandpa, please! That money has got to last us all the way to California."

"Anybody else want to get in on this?" Roy asks, looking at the spectators on the benches.

The cowboys form a line to place their bets. The money is counted out and put in Roy's hat, which he sets on the side rail.

"Get up there and play!" he says.

I stomp up to the pool table.

"We're gonna end up broke," I tell him.

Red Feather edges me out by a hair on the lag. I rack up the rocks, watch him aim down his custom stick. Despite his sledgehammer break, no balls go in. I sink the first three balls fairly fast then call a four-five combo, sinking the 5-ball into the corner pocket. I chalk up, studying the layout. I can either sink the 6-ball with a bank shot then feather the 7-ball into the corner, leaving me with ducks at the eight and nine, or I can stall the six with a dogged bank shot and spin the cue ball into a lockup at the side rail. I take the second option, just to see Red Feather squirm.

But he doesn't squirm. Shooting almost straight down, he spins the cue ball clean around the 9-ball. The cue taps the 6-ball, sending it into the corner pocket. I am amazed. A trick shot like that would take a hundred hours of practice to get down even half right.

He clears the table, then stands there scratching his crotch. He winks at one of the cowboys on the bench.

Don't count your money yet, buddy-ro, I think, as I rack up the rocks.

In the next game, Red Feather runs one through seven, but he's a little off on a carom and scratches on the 8-ball. Setting the cue ball up in the kitchen, I sink the eight and nine fast and win the second game.

Roy cackles, takes a swig out of his flask. "Told you she was good."

"She got lucky is all," Red Feather says with a shrug.

He racks them up and I break, but nothing goes in. He studies the stack a moment, then sinks the 1-ball, setting him up for puppies at the two and three. I feel sweat pop out on my face. I've got a nervous tic in my left eye. Something about Red Feather bugs me; what is it? Watching him, I suddenly figure out what it is. He reminds me of Bob Conari. He is not only big and pot-bellied like Bob, he has the same look in his eyes, like he thinks the whole world is here just to serve him. I feel my face flush and my knees tremble.

Whoa, I think. Be cool.

But it's too late, I dog my chance to win this game by scratching on the 7-ball. Put too much spin on the cue. I lose the next one, too—dogging a bank shot at the 5-ball after Red Feather distracts me with a loud burp. Two more wins, and Red Feather and his boys got our money.

When Red Feather sinks the 9-ball on the break, I'm beginning to think this guy has all the cheese, that this is just more bad luck for us that started with the knocking engine. Didn't Cody almost get bit by a snake today?

Roy calls time out. He takes me over to a bench where he can keep an eye on the hatful of money and talk to me, too.

"Pull yourself together, Jenna. Take some deep breaths. Get your center back. You've taken out players as good as him. Remember that ace you beat in St. Pete, the one with all the rings? He was packing some serious weight, and you beat him. And that skinny black guy in Mobile? We fleeced him, too, and he was no better than this clown. You're gonna beat him tonight. You can do it."

"I know I can do it." I shut my eyes tight, trying to believe it.

To calm down I go up to the front and buy a 7-Up from Mom. I sit at the counter, sipping the drink and picturing myself winning—a little trick Roy taught me. He believes the key to winning is in the mind. "The mind can do miracles," he says. "How do you think Jesus healed the lepers?"

"Your grandpa's got plenty of confidence," Mom says. "Been playing long?"

"Few years."

"The old man's been at it a lot longer than that." She jerks her head toward the back, causing rolls of fat to ripple everywhere, like a waterbed.

"I told him I wanted to leave."

"Sure you did, girlie."

I look at the sign on the wall behind her next to the beer and soft-drink cooler: All guns left with Mom. No exceptions!

"What do you do if you catch someone in here with a gun?"

"Sit on his face," Mom says.

I drink the 7-Up down fast and go back to the table, whistling the tune to "When The Saints Go Marching In," for luck. I rack up, and Red Feather sinks the 1-ball on the break. After sinking two through six, he tries to cut the 7-ball into the corner pocket but he shoots a hair too hard, and the seven bounces out of the pocket—the tightest one on the table.

"She's got his ass now," I hear Roy say.

Red Feather gives Roy a hateful look.

I sink the seven and call a combo on the 8-ball, putting the money ball in the side pocket.

"Yahoo!" Roy says, clapping.

Red Feather's face is flushed. He doesn't look so cocky now.

I sink the 5-ball on the break. Feeling lucky, I clear the table, then flash him a smile.

He doesn't smile back.

In the next game I dog a lockup at the nine after chalking up. The tip of the stick just slides off the cue ball. Someone slimed the chalk with spit, a nasty trick I've seen before.

Leaning over the table, his fat belly mashed against the side rail, Red Feather sinks the nine off a six-eight combo.

I've got to beat him, I think, as I get the chalk off a nearby table. My heart is beating too fast. Be calm, I think. You can do it. You can win.

I win the next game with a one-two combination on the 9-ball. I win the one after that, too, after Red Feather is a hair off on a bank shot at the seven. By now I've figured out he isn't as cool as he acts. He plays fine when he's winning, but he cracks under pressure. Soon I am four games ahead, and Red Feather is popping his hairy knuckles, licking his lips, wiping his forehead with his sleeve.

The problem was my mindset, I think, as I watch him rack up the ivories. I just had to get my center back. He thinks he's a real man of the cloth, but I can beat him as long as I maintain my mental control.

I sink eight balls on a string, tuning out Red Feather's loud burps and sudden digs at his crotch. I am taking aim at the money ball when three of Red Feather's stakehorses step between him and Roy. Before I can shoot, Red Feather unzips his pants and flashes his thing above the corner pocket.

He gets me so rattled I miss the shot.

"My, my," Red Feather says, zipping up. Sick and mad, too, I watch him lean over and take aim at the yellow-striped ball. It's a lockup, just a little cut on the corner of the 9-ball will put it in. I could make it in my sleep.

"Aieeeeeeeooouuu!" Roy cries, popping up from the bench like a Ninja.

Red Feather is a hair off on the cut, missing the shot. "Son of a bitch!"

Roy is hopping up and down, rubbing his hip. "Something stung me!"

Quickly, I lean over and sink the 9-ball. I see a cowboy's mouth drop open.

"What the frick is this?" Red Feather says. "What the frick's going on?"

Roy's jump has taken him close to the side rail. He grabs up the money hat, puts it on his head.

"I'm allergic to wasps," he says, rubbing his hip. "Poison goes straight to my heart."

"Ain't no wasps in here," one of the cowboys says. But I see him inspecting the bench.

"Let's go, Grandpa," I say, taking Roy's hand. "I got to get you to a doctor."

As we go by the counter, Mom says, "What's all the commotion about?"

"Grandpa got stung!"

Outside, on the sidewalk, I look back at the pool hall. It's dark out now, and the streetlights are on. We walk fast down the street. I keep looking back and see the door of the pool hall open just as we turn the corner.

We cut down an alley, turn the corner and walk fast to the next block, ducking into a Kentucky Fried. While Roy is ordering a bucket of chicken, I look outside and see a truck go by with a bunch of cowboys in the back. One of them is Red Feather.

I tell Roy this and he calls us a cab from the pay phone by the door. We wait for the cab in a back booth.

"That was the closest one I've had yet," I say.

"He ain't nothing," Roy says. "Damn slimeball."

"How long you reckon they'll look for us?"

"They ain't gonna do nothing but go home and scratch their little mad places."

On the way out to the Texaco, we lay into the bucket of chicken. Roy gives the cabby a drumstick.

"Where you folks from?" he asks.

"Back east," Roy says.

"Planning on staying in Delphia?"

"It's a fine little town," Roy says, "but we're on our way to California."

"Lots of people have left this town for somewhere else," the cabbie says, more to himself than to us.

After he pulls into the Texaco, the cab driver looks at me and says, "Did you know there's over six hundred people living in Los Angeles who believe they're Jesus Christ? "

"We're gonna be living on a farm," I tell him.

Roy hands him a twenty. "How about waiting here a minute?"

We go back to the truck. Roy unlocks the door and Cody jumps out on the ground, bouncing up and down like a basketball.

"Smell the chicken, huh." I tear some meat off a breast and toss it to him. He catches it in midair.

Roy takes a whiz behind the station, then comes back and sits down on the grate. In the station's neon light his beard looks like the angel hair you hang on a Christmas tree.

"Ready to sleep in a motel?"

"You bet!"

"Get your things together."

"We'll have to sneak Cody in."

"Won't be the first time."

We pack a suitcase, lock up the truck, then go back to the taxi.

"Where's the best motel in town?" Roy asks.

"That would be the Loralee, out on West Boulevard."

"Let's go."

Cody is sitting between us, his eyes on the bucket of chicken. He whines, wiggles, barks. Roy gives him a piece of chicken. "Cody, you got the life."

"We'll all have the life in California," I say.

"You bet, sweetheart." Roy gives my hand a squeeze.

Later that night, after I've had a hot shower, Roy tells me he doesn't want us to hustle anymore. He says I should just play pool as a sport.

"But, Roy, I like being a shark. You said I'm a natural."

"It's the wrong kind of life for you."

"What's that supposed to mean? Just because that dumb jerk pulled out his thing?"

"The game has changed, Jenna. There's too many slimeballs out there now. Scumbags who'll cut your heart out for a dollar. Ain't a decent environment for a twelve-year-old girl."

"I can deal with it."

"Well, I can't. And I damn sure can't live my life over again through you." Roy picks up the remote and switches on the TV. "We need to get a move on, anyway. You should be in school."

"School! Yuck."

To cool off, I take Cody and go down to sit in a chair by the pool. There's a girl and boy in there, swimming. "I don't care about the money," I tell Cody. "What I really like is beating jerks like Red Feather who think they're God's gift to the world."

Cody isn't paying attention. He is looking at the pool where the boy and girl are kissing. They kiss so long I wonder how they can breathe. Finally, they break apart, climb out of the pool, and walk into the shadows. For some reason this makes me cry, and once I get started I can't seem to stop.

"Those are just lovebirds," I tell Cody. I try to picture my True Love, but my mind lingers on the boy and girl. I wonder where they are from, where they are going. The pool's lights go off suddenly, and I can see the moon's image in the water, changing shapes like a reflection in a hall of mirrors. I have a tight, fluttery feeling in my heart. Raising my eyes I see, in the moonlight, a white owl flying overhead. It passes by so quickly I wonder if I only imagined it. I pull Cody close to me, hoping it is a sign of good luck to come.

# A Good Gravedigger

After Jeanine and me busted up I was knocked so flat I got a job helping Holt and Lysander Waller dig graves. The Wallers are pure-T legends with funeral home directors around here. They know where every cemetery is within seven counties, and they've buried near 'bout half the folks in them. Although they're both on the high side of sixty they go full-tilt boogie from sunup till dark, and they just about run me ragged. I come home nights with blisters the size of half dollars on my palms, my body aching like I been beat, my ears ringing with that holy-roller music the Waller brothers listen to all day long, mostly tapes by the Reverend Sweet Daddy Grace and his Tuscaloosa Choir. My head hits the pillow, and I'm gone for the night. But that's all right; my job with the Wallers takes my mind off Jeanine.

My present trouble commences with a man named Emmett Buxley, a jackleg plumber down in Chickasaw County. We bury him on Monday, and on Thursday, after a big rain, Holt tells me we got to go back and bury him again on account of he floated up out of the ground.

Being that Emmett Buxley's grave plot is in betwixt some water oaks, Lysander can't get his backhoe in there, so Holt and me have to work with shovels. It's hard, hateful work in marshy ground all snaky with roots, and the whole time Holt and me are digging, Lysander, who has a bad back, is sitting in the air-conditioned truck, listening to Sweet Daddy Grace and sipping cool water from a thermos.

That night, after I clean myself up, I relax on my sofa watching TV and drinking a cold beer. Although my body aches and my hands are raw, I am feeling right good and decent because I know Emmett is now deep in the ground due to my hard labor, and him and his family can rest in peace.

Before I turn in I take a spin down Main Street, and who do I see but Jeanine riding in Hooty Tillett's red Firebird convertible. Pain convulses my heart like a holy visitation. I am vexed and sore as a burnt weasel, but I realize there is nothing I can do about the fact that Hooty is drawing water out of her well. It's a free country, and Jeanine and me agreed to that sort of thing when we parted.

Resolving to break her hold on me I take some girls out, but I can't get my mind off Jeanine. I keep remembering the low, husky sound of her voice, her honeysuckle smell, and the way she'd clamp me in her love-vise and holler for glory. I even picture her one night when me and a little honey are shooting the rapids in the back seat of my old Chevy. She is a wildcat, barely sixteen and already hot as a firecracker, but all I can do is hang on tight, pining away for Jeanine.

I mail her pictures back to her. I throw out every card she ever sent me, and give away or throw out all her gifts, including the T-shirt with "Jeanine's Lover Man" printed on it. I am determined to erase her presence from my life.

As time goes on I get to seeing Sweet Little Sixteen every weekend, and although I still dream about Jeanine, I feel my heartache easing some. I try to stay busy and concentrate on being a good gravedigger. It's a hard, dirty job but somebody's got to do it, is the Waller brothers' philosophy on this. They been at it forty-some years and have buried every kind of person there is. Black and white, young and old, rich, poor and in between, not to mention their own mama and daddy and a slew of other kin. I take my cue from them and try not to think too much about the departed. It's just a job, a way for me to eat, pay my rent, and stay so busy I won't have to think about Jeanine.

In June, a tropical storm blows in off the ocean, and the next thing I know, the Waller brothers and me are back down in Chickasaw County, burying Emmett again. We dig that grave so deep Lysander has got to throw down a rope so we can climb out. By then, I'm wore down to a frazzle.

"You reckon he gonna stay buried now?" Lysander says, when I get in the truck. Ain't even broke a sweat today, still smells of soap from his morning shower.

I am so vexed and wearified I don't even answer.

That night, I drive down to the 7-Eleven for a six-pack, and I see Hooty Tillett sitting in his red convertible by the gas pumps, combing his hair and admiring himself in the rearview mirror. Inside the store, leaning over the ice cream cooler, wearing pink shortie shorts and a T-shirt so thin you can see her nipples shining through, is my old flame, Jeanine.

"I got the pictures," she says, all pouty. "You didn't have to send 'em back."

"I was just cleaning up and thought you might want 'em."

"You look a little puny in the eyes. Been eating right?"

"I been working my ass off," I tell her. "Spent all day digging a big hole in the ground."

"What you digging a hole in the ground for?" she asks, pressing her titties against my arm. "Looking for treasure?"

"I was burying a man if you must know."

Hooty is leaning on his horn now.

"I got to go," Jeanine says. "You take care of yourself now, hear?'

"I'll be all right."

"Bye-bye, Gus."

Her honeysuckle smell lingers in my nose as I watch her walk in those shortie shorts out to Hooty's car, open the door, and slide in. Pain cuts my heart like a razor. I am knocked so flat I go home, lay down on the living room floor, and cry like a whipped dog.

Jeanine was my first love, and the sight of her getting into Hooty's Firebird slices me to the bone, especially considering the source of our breakup. Jeanine flat out said she needed a man with a more solid future. She said she loved me to distraction, but being that I didn't have a real career-type job other than helping my uncle frame houses when the weather was good, she was afraid a life with me would mean scrimping and scratching just to get by, and she had her sights fixed on a fancy brick home with a shiny new Chevrolet sitting out front and a TV in every room. "You mean the world to me, honey," she said. "But facts is facts. You ain't got much more than a pot to piss in, and the road ahead looks mighty rough and rocky."

Jeanine said if I could get some direction to my life she'd like to pick up where we was leaving off. But I figured it was best to make a clean break, being as it was clear I wasn't good enough for her. "I really want you to be happy, Jeanine," I said. "And if a rich man is what you need, then I hope you'll find one who will treat you like a queen. Just think of me every so often and remember the good times we shared."

We both cried then, and when we kissed seemed like Jeanine was trying to stick her tongue all the way down to my tonsils. "I'll never forget you, Gus," she told me. "Baby, you got the finest loving this side of Heaven."

That right there is the best thing anyone ever said to me. I want that placed on my tombstone.

I even talk to the Wallers about it one day, although only in general terms. Lysander says he's seen worse things than that on tombstones. Then him and Holt get to talking about the worst epitaphs they ever seen. Holt recollects an exterminator whose tombstone read, "There's no bugs in Heaven." And a cab driver whose epitaph was "My meter ran out, but the Master's meter never stops running." Lysander says his all-time worst was "My heart may be full of worms, but my soul has gone to God."

"I knowed that feller, too," Lysander adds. "He was a boozer that beat his wife."

"Words don't mean nothing," Holt says. "Words won't help you at all."

By the middle of July, my hands are hard and callused from using a pickax and shovel, and I got muscles galore. I am out in the sun so much I am near 'bout as brown as the Waller brothers.

Meanwhile, Sweet Little Sixteen is getting all moon-eyed, wanting me to buy her a friendship ring. Talk like this makes me break out in hives. "Whassamatter, baby," she says, "you got fleas?"

"Hell no, I ain't got fleas. What do I look like, a dog?"

"Well, you itching like one."

"Must be something I ate."

" 'Maters makes me break out all over," she says. "You been eating 'maters?"

"Not lately."

"Might be the heat." She runs her fingers along the inside of my thigh. "You know they're having a big sale on rings right now over at the mall. Let's ride over there and check 'em out."

"Seems like we just met," I tell her. "Let's wait a while before we talk about rings."

She smiles and says, "No problem," but I can tell by the way her mouth is set she means to wear me down. Later, I catch her staring at me in a manner that reminds me of a cat staring at a fish in a bowl. "What's eating you, Gus?" she asks. "Got some old girlfriend on your mind?"

"Must be heartburn," I say. "I need to lay off that Mexican food."

Sunk low in the melancholy depths of my sorrow, I volunteer for Saturday work with the Wallers, who seem to appreciate my interest. I attack the ground like a man possessed. Even catch myself singing along with the Tuscaloosa Choir on "Jesus Is the Friend You Need."

In August, Chickasaw County has a flash flood, and after the waters recede, Holt gives me the news: Emmett has done ascended from the ground again. This time he has floated down to the gas station at the crossroads.

"Lord God in Heaven," I say. "That man won't stay buried."

"We gonna put him deep this time," says Holt. "We gonna put him halfway down to China."

"I don't see where it's our responsibility," I say.

"We guarantee our work," Lysander says.

I start to say something else, but Holt turns up the volume on the Rev. Sweet Daddy Grace, who is singing "There's a Power Greater Than You."

Being that we got four new graves to dig, it's after dark before we get Emmett Buxley back in the ground. We dump a load of gravel on his casket, hoping that will keep him down for good.

Riding home, I am so dogged tired I fall asleep on Lysander's shoulder.

I am dreaming of a rat with foot-long whiskers when Holt shakes me awake. "We just about at your house, Gus."

We're at the stoplight just before the turnoff to my house. Ahead I see Hooty's red convertible with Jeanine all snuggled up against his side. "She used to be my girl," I say.

Holt and Lysander study her with interest.

"She riding in a sporty-looking vehicle," Lysander says.

"Look like she done forgot all about you, Gus," Holt adds.

They drop me off at my house, and I limp into the kitchen, open the fridge, and drain a twelve-ounce beer. I am sick to my soul from seeing Jeanine scrunched up against Hooty like they was Siamese twins. As I set the empty on the table I am struck by a strange coincidence: during the past three months the only times I've laid eyes on Jeanine and Hooty is right after I've reburied Emmett Buxley. "Now that gives me a right uneasy feeling," I say, and I reach for another beer.

I toss and turn in my bed till after midnight, brooding on this unholy connection before I finally drift off to sleep.

Sometime before dawn I wake up hearing the telephone ringing. I get up and walk into the living room to answer it.

"Hello," says this voice. "How you doing, Gus?"

"Who's this?"

"Emmett."

"Emmett who?"

"Emmett Buxley."

"Only Emmett Buxley I ever heard tell of is from down Chickasaw way."

"I'm him."

Suddenly I've got a major case of the heebie-jeebies. A feeling on my skin like a giant moth is brushing me with its wings.

"What the hell you talking on the phone for, Emmett? You dead!"

"But as you can see, I won't stay buried."

"I can't deal with this, Emmett. What you want to haunt me for? I ain't never done nothing to you, 'cept try to give you a decent burial."

"What did you let that girl give you the brushoff for, Gus?"

"Girl? What girl?"

"You know who."

"You talking about Jeanine?"

"You give that girl up too easy, boy. You want her, you need to fight for her."

"I want her, but what can I do? Hooty Tillett is assistant manager at Burger King. He's done put a down payment on a new double-wide mobile home, and, besides, he's got that Firebird."

"You got your ass in a sling, boy. Listen, you want that girl?"

"Yeah, but—"

"Ain't no buts about it. Go after her, then! Do whatever it takes to get her back. You a damned fool if you don't."

There is a click, and then all I hear is the dial tone.

"Emmett!" I shout into the receiver. "You stay in the ground, you hear me?"

I go back to bed, but sleep is out of the question. I can't get that phone call out of my mind. Was that a haint on the phone or someone playing a joke? If it was Emmett, what's he so interested in my personal business for? And why do I keep seeing Hooty and Jeanine every time he floats up out of the ground?

I got no answer for these questions. But I puzzle over them until I feel like a dog chasing its own tail around.

Come daylight, I get up, make coffee, and sit on my front steps, listening to the birds sing. Won't be long before the Wallers are turning into my driveway. We got five graves to dig today, one way down in Pike County.

"It was just a dream," I say. But a voice inside my head says, *That won't no dream. That there was a call from a man who has passed into the Great Beyond and therefore sees and knows things you can only guess at.*

That phone call has not only shook me up, it has also made me realize I did give Jeanine up too easy. Why did I do that? I wonder. Why didn't I fight harder for her?

That's a serious question that needs answering, and I'll get to it by and by, but right now I need to concentrate on pulling myself together before the Wallers arrive. They ain't going to have time for no high-strung, fretful gravedigger. No way. The Wallers expect a hard day's work for a full day's pay. They ain't going to want to hear talk of a phone call from a man done buried four times now, a man I hope and pray will stay gone.

# Love to the Spirits

The first time I ever laid eyes on Leon Streker I said to myself, "This one is trouble." Dudley, the orderly, was pushing him down the hall in a wheelchair, Mr. Streker winking at the ladies as he rolled by. "Howdy, hon," he said. "Hey there, doll." You could tell he might have been a halfway decent-looking man once, maybe back in his youth before he started living a wanton life, but he was ugly as a pirate now, with his gaunt, pockmarked face and black eyes darting this way and that like he was looking for something to steal.

They brought him in from the county jail because he had inoperable cancer, and they didn't know where else to put him. I learned this from Dudley, who had overheard the administrator, Glenda Aimis, talking about Mr. Streker to one of the nurses. Ms. Aimis put him in room 326 on our wing.

A few hours after he arrived, I heard a commotion in the hall. I stepped out and nearly collided with Mr. Streker in his wheelchair, whose hands were moving furiously on the wheels. Close behind him was George Whitehurst, his neighbor in 328.

My first thought was the place was on fire.

They didn't slow down at the front desk, but turned sharp to the left and disappeared around the corner, going toward the rec room and cafeteria. Helen Steadman, the head nurse, jumped up and went after them.

Couldn't be fire, I thought, or else they'd have gone out the front door. What in the world was going on?

They soon came back around the front desk, followed by Nurse Steadman.

"No more of that racing now," she said, speaking to them like two unruly boys.

Mr. Streker and Mr. Whitehurst rolled back down the hall, their faces flushed, unpenitent.

"I was ahead when she captured us," Mr. Whitehurst said to me as he went by.

Mr. Whitehurst's nickname here at Hillhaven Manor is the Hermit because he spends so much time in his room with the door shut. He's seventy-five and wears two hearing aids. He was here when I arrived three years ago, and as far as I knew he had never caused a speck of trouble until that day.

Leon Streker had been here less than twenty-four hours, and the bad feeling I had about him was already bearing fruit.

"What do you think of Leon Streker?" Grace Sullivan asked later in the rec room, where we were doing our daily calisthenics.

"Who?" I asked, although I knew exactly whom she was talking about.

"The new man, in three-twenty-six." Grace's room was across from his.

"You mean the jailbird?"

"Jailbird?"

I told her what Dudley had told me.

"What was he in jail for?"

"I have no idea," I said. "But judging by his looks it was something despicable."

"I guess I shouldn't have loaned him that money."

"Grace!"

"He said he was expecting a check and he'd pay me back as soon as it arrived."

"How much did you give him?"

"Ten dollars."

"You might as well kiss that money goodbye."

"He seemed so sincere," Grace said.

"That's what Eve said about the snake," I said.

That evening he came in to see me. Of course he didn't knock.

"Hello," he said. "My name's Leon, and I'm new here. What's that you're watching on TV?"

"Do you always enter people's rooms without knocking first?"

"Guess I've forgotten some of the things my mama taught me."

"You should always take time for manners, Mr. Streker."

"I can see my reputation has preceded me." He smiled, showing broken, stained teeth. His eyes darted around my room until they alighted on the photo of Danny on the wall.

"Nice looking boy. Your son?"

"Did you come by for a special reason, Mr. Streker?"

"As a matter of fact I did. When I saw you in the cafeteria today, I couldn't help noticing the way you carry yourself. Your bearing shows dignity, character, and quite a bit of pride. Those are refreshing qualities to see, especially in a nursing home. I wanted to tell you now because they tell me I don't have long to live. Therefore, I don't believe in holding things in."

"Your compliment is duly noted," I said. "Now, if you'll excuse me, I'm missing my show."

"Enjoy your show, Ruth." As he was shuffling out, he added, "And have a pleasant evening."

Despite my efforts to warn others about Mr. Streker, he managed to charm the other residents here at Hillhaven Manor. Nearly everyone seemed to like him, at least those still able to form an opinion. He was the most gregarious con man I've ever seen, rolling up and down the halls in his wheelchair (although he seemed to have no problem walking), visiting residents in their rooms. He bathed everyone with this relentlessly obnoxious good will, even those too far gone to be influenced by it, like old Mrs. Morton in 213. Twice a day, they wheel her out to the hall, where she sits and babbles at everyone who passes.

"Evening, ma'am," Mr. Streker would say. "It's good to be alive."

Mrs. Morton is a member of a group here that I call the Vegetables, who have lost the power of thought. The worst of these are the Whiners—like Mrs.

Baumgardner in room 314. "Help me," she'll cry, over and over. "Somebody please help me."

I used to go in to see her. She's in her nineties, wrinkled as a lizard. "What's wrong, honey," I'd ask. "What's wrong?"

She was beautiful once. In a photograph of her on the wall, taken when she was young, she has a sculpted face framed by dark curls, a heart-shaped mouth, laughing eyes. And now, age has brought her to this, a whining bag of bones with a lizard's face.

Ask her what's wrong, all she can do is point and talk like an infant.

What's wrong with her is what's wrong with all of us here at Hillhaven Manor: we have one foot in the grave, and we're waiting to take that last step.

The real trouble I sensed in Mr. Streker came in the form of a photo-copied paper I found slid under my door a few days after his arrival. The sheet bore this message:

*Send a message to a loved one in the spirit world.*
*Only 50 cents per word.*
*See Leon Streker, room 326.*
*(I am terminally ill.)*

I showed the notice to Helen Steadman, at the front desk.

"Have you seen this?" I asked.

"Yes," she said, shaking her head. "That Mr. Streker."

"There ought to be a rule against this."

"I suppose he could claim freedom of speech."

"He's a vicious hustler, Helen. Trying to make money off the loss of loved ones."

I threw the paper in the wastebasket. No one is stupid enough to fall for that, I thought.

But my assumption was wrong.

At lunch, Thelma Griggs and Nellie Sewell said they were considering using his "service" to send messages to their departed husbands.

"I can't believe you all would let yourself be duped by that jailbird," I said.

"Well, he doesn't have long to live," Nellie said. "I've heard he has liver cancer."

"What makes you think he'll be able to deliver messages to your loved ones for you?"

"He might not be able to," Thelma said. "But what if he can? It's worth the money just to have the chance to send a message to Ralph."

"You ought to think about it, too, Ruth," Nellie said. "What do you have to lose except a little money?"

"I don't have any loved ones where he's going," I said.


One by one, they fell for it. Like children following the Pied Piper.

First Thelma bought a message to send to her husband. Then Nellie sent her husband and sister messages. Grace, Luella, and June all bought messages, too.

When Bill Latimer, my next-door neighbor, came in to get my help writing a message to his wife, I tried to talk him out of it.

"I can't believe you're falling for that con man's scheme."

"What makes you think it's a scheme?"

"It's painfully obvious that he's just trying to hustle your money."

"He is dying, isn't he?"

"I suppose so, but what's that got to do with it?"

"I just thought he might be able to—talk to Laura for me."

"Why are you coming to me, Bill?"

"You used to be a teacher, didn't you?"

"Librarian."

"Well, that's like a teacher, isn't it?"

With his plump face, double chin, and bald head, Bill reminded me of a big baby. Men, I thought. They're so good at being helpless. It's their number two talent, next to stirring up trouble.

"What do you want to say to your wife?"

"I want to tell her I miss her."

"Why don't you write that down, then?"

"I can't write very good. It's my arthritis."

I held out my hand for his pen and notebook. "Tell me what you want to say."

He gave them to me, but then he just sat there, biting his lip.

"I don't know how to get started, Ruth."

"Pretend she's in the next room and you want me to tell her something."

He shut his eyes. His lips quivered.

"Dear Laura, I miss you something awful. Life has been so hard without you. I can't wait to see you again, wherever you are."

He opened his eyes, waited for me to finish writing.

"How does that sound?"

"Do you really want to tell her how hard your life has been? There's nothing she can do about that, Bill. A simple 'I miss you' seems adequate."

"All right. Cut that part out then."

"Now, you can also cut 'wherever you are.' It doesn't seem necessary. How's this? 'I miss you and can't wait to see you again.' "

"That's good. I'd also like to tell her that our daughter, Janet, had another child, a boy. See, Laura died before he was born, and she never got a chance to see him. He's ten now."

I said it as I wrote it: " 'Janet had a boy. He's ten.' What else?"

"I'd love for you to see him and be able to talk to him."

"Maybe she can see him."

"Do you think she can? I mean—you know—see him?"

"I can't answer that question, but I think you might want to reconsider your statement, 'I'd love for you to see him and be able to talk to him.' "

"Why?"

"You're wishing for something impossible, at least in this life."

"I see what you mean."

"Why don't you just tell her how you feel about him?"

He closed his eyes again.

"He's a beautiful boy who everyone says has your eyes, and I'm very proud of him."

"Good! Do you want to end it now?"

"I am looking forward to being reunited with you. Love, Bill."

"Very good. But I'm crossing out 'I am.' That saves a dollar."

I counted the words. "Forty-six. That's twenty-three dollars. I think we can cut this down somewhere."

"It's fine. Let's just go with it like it is." Tears glistened in Bill's eyes. He squeezed my hand. "Ruth, I can't tell you how much I appreciate this."

After he left, I sat there, marveling at how gullible people are when they are old and lonely.

At least I saved him some money, I thought. Leon Streker would milk him dry if he could.

That night I dreamed about my son, Danny—the first dream I'd had about him in years. He was just a toddler, and I was giving him a bath. The dream was so vivid it woke me up.

All that talk about spirits is making me jumpy, I thought. I'll be glad when that Leon Streker is gone. Maybe then things will get back to normal around here.

Mr. Streker came in to see me again, in his wheelchair this time. Still didn't knock.

"Afternoon, Ruth. Get my notice?"

"I got it," I said.

"Have you thought about sending someone a message?"

"Now why would I want to do that?"

"Don't you want to send your love to someone in the spirit world?"

"I think you're the lowest kind of snake, Mr. Streker. Coming in here and preying on these gullible people."

His eyes widened in an exaggerated attempt to look injured.

"I'm providing a legitimate service for a modest fee."

"Is that right?"

"Yes. You can send a message to anyone in any part of the civilized world, using Western Union. But how can you get a message to a departed loved one other than using a service like mine? Not only that, it goes without saying that I'm giving my life to carry out my end of the bargain."

"Why do you have to charge money? Seems to me if your heart was in the right place, you'd provide your service for free."

"I'd like to do that. Unfortunately, I need the money too bad not to charge a fee."

"If you need money, why can't you get help from your family?"

"It's true my family is financing the cost of my stay here, but that's due to their desire to maintain their good name. Their sudden generosity occurred after a story about my plight appeared in the hometown newspaper. On a personal basis, my family wouldn't shoo buzzards off me if I was lying dead in the road."

"What did you do to them?"

"Disgraced them. My mother, bless her soul, is deceased, but my father owns a string of clothing stores. My brother is an attorney. My sister married a doctor. My father wanted me to sell suits, but I ran away and joined the circus. I started out taking care of the elephants and tigers, but I dreamed of being more than a shoveller of elephant and tiger dung. I was lucky enough to become an apprentice to Hurlo Amarati, the great sword swallower, who taught me the secrets of swallowing things. I started out with string, then went on to wires, coat hangers, sticks, and, finally, swords. I could put ten down my throat at one time. I became as good as Hurlo himself, before I developed this problem with a certain muscle, a little flap that holds back food. This put an end to my career in entertainment, a field which, I'd like to point out, offers very little in the way of financial security."

"Working for a circus hardly seems like a reason for your family to disown you, especially when you're—ill."

"You don't know my family. They're pillars of the community. They disapprove of me because I rebelled against their stuffy little world. My sister has never forgiven me for this tattoo." He pulled up the sleeve of his pajamas, exposing an unpleasant tattoo on his bicep: a fire-breathing dragon with a forked tongue.

"What were you in jail for?"

"My most recent offense was for vagrancy. Do you know that in our state there's a law against being poor? It's a law that allows the police to arrest you if you have less than one dollar in your pocket. Do you see the colossal injustice in this—to be jailed simply for being poor?"

"You could find another job besides swallowing swords."

"I've had them. I've worked in factories, painted houses, cleaned chimneys, taken up tickets at the movies, but those jobs have never made me happy, so I've gone on to the next one, looking for—" Mr. Streker paused, groping to complete his thought.

"A free ride?"

"No! The next perfect moment, that's the best way I can put it. See, most people spend their lives trying to find happiness in big things—promotions, marriages, social positions, financial success. But since those areas never worked out for me, I've learned to find happiness in little things. I especially enjoy seeing someone's face light up in a smile. Ever watched someone who was frowning suddenly smile? Watch."

He made his ugly face even uglier by scowling; then, slowly, the muscles relaxed into a smile.

"See the transformation! It's like the sun breaking through a storm cloud."

In your case, Mr. Streker, I thought, it doesn't help your appearance much.

"Speaking of smiling," he said, "I've never seen you smile."

"What's there to smile about in a mausoleum like this?"

"You're alive. And you have your wits about you, unlike some less fortunate people around here. You have good food, a warm place to sleep out of the rain."

"You call what they serve here 'good food'?"

"Compared to what I've been eating in jail it's fit for royalty. Know what they served us every morning at six A.M.?"

"I wouldn't know what they serve in jail, Mr. Streker."

"A bowl of salty water with a few beans floating around it and two pieces of stale bread. Every morning, the same thing. The jailer insisted on calling it 'soup and sandwich.' "

"The fact remains that you're taking advantage of people in a helpless position, and that makes you a reptile in my book, Mr. Streker. A common, lowdown reptile. Now, if you'll excuse me, I'd like to take a nap. I'm getting a headache."

"I'm sorry you have such a negative attitude about me. But I believe your real problem is that you're afraid I might actually have something to offer you. If I were a praying man, I'd say a prayer for you. But since I'm not I'll just say bye-bye for now."

After he left I turned out the light and lay down. I could feel my heart pounding. "You're living in a dream," I said, "if you think you have anything I need."

I couldn't sleep. I got up and turned on the light. I sat in my chair, looking at the photo of Danny on the wall. It was taken during his senior year, when he was a star quarterback for his high school team. That was one of the best years in Danny's life. It was also one of the happiest times in my marriage. Lawrence and I were doing a lot of things together. Going on picnics, vacations, and to all of Danny's athletic events. He played football, basketball, ran track, excelled at everything. He had the third highest grade point average in his senior class, quite an accomplishment in view of his athletic activity. Two days before he was to graduate he and a group of his friends went hiking in the mountains. There was some drinking involved, some clowning around. Danny slipped off a stone wall and fell three hundred feet. He was buried the day after graduation.

Two years later, Lawrence, a professor of history at Carolina, left me for one of his graduate students. They later had a child, a daughter I've never seen. Lawrence is seventy-four and a victim of Alzheimer's. His sister told me he can't remember his daughter's name.

Dudley, the orderly, was making my bed while I sat in the chair by the stand.

"Dudley, have you been drinking?"

"No, ma'am."

"What is that I smell then?"

"Might be mouthwash."

"I've smelled mouthwash before, young man."

"They're putting new things in mouthwash these days, Mrs. Cantor."

Finishing up the bed, he hurried out of my room, although he usually stayed and talked awhile.

I knew Dudley was not the type of young man to drink on the job—not without some corrupting influence. I immediately suspected the source of that influence, too. Lately, Dudley had been spending far too much time in Mr. Streker's room with the door closed.

Later that morning I walked by Mr. Streker's room and heard the two of them laughing in there. I hated to be a tattletale, but I went up to the nursing station and told Helen she ought to pay a visit to 326. "Something strange is going on," I said.

"That Mr. Streker," she said, shaking her head. "All right, Ruth, I'll check on him."

I visited Grace in her room, so I could have a clear view of Mr. Streker's room. I saw Helen knock once, then go in and shut the door.

She was in there no more than two minutes, and when Dudley came out he was hanging his head. Nurse Steadman came out next, scowling.

Whatever they were doing, she caught them, I thought, with a jolt of joy.

And that's a rare gem in this place.

"They were gambling," Grace said. "They had the cards and the money on the table when she walked in. Dudley got a warning this time, but Mrs. Aimis said if it happens again he's gone."

Grace had heard what happened from another one of the orderlies, who had overheard Mrs. Aimis talking to Dudley in her office.

"Been anybody else but Dudley she'd have fired him outright," Thelma said.

"He's on probation," Grace said. "I hope he doesn't get fired. He's such a sweet boy."

"The fault lies with Mr. Streker," I said, "for spreading his evil net over Dudley." It was killing me not to mention the alcohol I had smelled on Dudley's breath, but I didn't want to get him in more trouble.

"He's a live wire, that Mr. Streker," Nellie said. "Know what he said to me yesterday?"

"I can't imagine."

"He said I had nice buns. Can you believe that?"

"The nerve," I said.

"No one has said anything like that to me in years. Nice buns."

"That man is a menace," I said. "He should be back in jail."

"Ruth," Thelma said, "did he tell you the joke about the homosexual camels?"

"I don't care to hear it," I said.

"It's a hoot," Thelma said. "But I'd hate to tell it. It's so dirty."

"Did he tell you the one about the preacher and the organist?" Isabelle said.

"Oh, my, yes," Nellie said, blushing. "That was awful."

"That man," Thelma said, shaking her head. "That man."

During the next few weeks, a steady stream of people fell victim to Mr. Streker's scam: not just the residents, but nurses, too, and visitors to Hillhaven Manor. I knew what he was doing with the money, too, at least part of it. He was drinking whiskey, which someone—I suspected Dudley— was sneaking in to him, since alcoholic beverages are strictly forbidden here. Grace said she smelled it on Mr. Streker's breath. Also, every evening he would roll up and down the halls singing songs like "Old Man River" and

"Good Night, Irene." He had a terrible voice, like a caterwauling tomcat. Whoever gave the man the idea he could sing? It just infuriated me to hear him singing his drunken songs, advertising his wantonness to the world. I was dying to go to Mrs. Aimis with my knowledge, and I refrained only out of concern for Dudley. Mrs. Aimis would fire him without hesitation if she learned he was an accomplice to Mr. Streker's ribald behavior.

I decided to deal with Dudley directly. I spoke to him one morning when he came in to get my breakfast tray.

"Dudley, you know you're on thin ice here, and it's all because of Mr. Streker,"

"Yes ma'am," he said.

"He's just pulling you down to his level when you gamble with him."

He looked truly contrite, but whether this was an act or not, I don't know.

"Dudley," I said softly, "do you know what would happen if you got caught sneaking liquor into him?"

Although Dudley was quiet, his hands trembled. He wouldn't look me in the eye.

"Why don't you just stop it? Stop it now, before it's too late."

"Yes, ma'am."

A few days later, after Mr. Streker's liquor supply ran out, I was happy to see that he ceased his evening serenades.


In my mail one morning there was a note from Lawrence's sister, along with a copy of his obituary notice.

Afterwards, I sat in my chair and looked out the window. I have a lovely view of a textile factory and, on the hill above, a cemetery. The sky was gray. As if in a film I saw scenes from our life together. I saw us dating, getting married, living in our first home, a cottage outside Nashville with weeping willows in the yard. Lawrence was doing his graduate work at Vanderbilt. Evenings we would walk down the road to a pond and feed the duck that stayed there. The duck would come quacking when it saw us. What did we name it? Sylvester. Sylvester the duck. I saw Lawrence's face when I told him I was pregnant. I saw Danny—as a baby, a toddler, a child. I saw us attending church, sitting on the swing on our porch, going camping, visiting both sets of Danny's grandparents. I saw Lawrence and Danny throwing the softball in the yard and fishing off that pier at the lake in the mountains where we vacationed many summers.

The scenes accelerated, like someone was fast-forwarding them on a VCR, until they became a blur, the billion moments of our lives together flashing by in a stream of light.

Then I was looking again at the factory again, the cemetery on the hill.

Suddenly, I had an overwhelming urge to hold Danny, to touch him, if only for a moment. The need was so strong I would have given my life just to hold him a moment. Oh my baby, where did you go?

I couldn't stop shaking as I considered how many people I had loved were dead. My grandparents, my parents. My brother. My aunts, uncles, many of my schoolmates. My son, and now his father, too, with whom I had shared a bed and a life for twenty-one years.

Is this all there is to life? I thought.

You begin with such promise, such hope. And you end up in a cubicle looking out the window at a factory, a graveyard.

Is this it?


"Come in, please," Mr. Streker said.

I pushed open his door and went into his room.

He was sitting in his wheelchair, looking out the window, his back to the door. When he turned toward me, I noticed his gaunt face was beginning to look cadaverous. His intense, black eyes had lit up with what appeared to be genuine warmth, however. "Why, hello, Ruth."

"I have a message," I said. "It's twenty-three words, which comes to eleven fifty. But I don't want to pay you for it."

He chewed on his thumbnail, his brow furrowed.

"I'll play you one game of seven-card stud," I said. "You win, I'll pay you double. I win, you deliver my message for free."

"Where did you learn to play poker?"

"I was young once, Mr. Streker."

He rolled over to the nightstand by his bed and got a deck of cards out of the drawer.

"Have a seat, Ruth."

I sat down at the table by the window. He wheeled up to the table and began shuffling the cards. He made them fall in a stream, from one hand to the other, like a waterfall; then he divided them into separate packs and arched them into the air, flowing them into a single pack again. He did this effortlessly, smiling at me with his black, larcenous eyes.

My message, on a sheet of notebook paper in my pocket, was to Danny. *My darling son, I love you more than ever and look forward to the time when I can see you again. Love, Mama.*

"Would you like to cut the deck?" he asked.

"Yes, I would." I cut it in four neat stacks, then put them all together.

"Seven card showdown," he said, picking up the deck. "Straight up okay?"

"Fine."

Mr. Streker dealt me a three of hearts, himself a five of diamonds. Next, I got a seven of clubs, he got a jack of hearts. Then I got an ace of spades. He got a six of clubs.

"Ace high," he said. "Would you like to do any other betting, Ruth?"

"One game. One bet."

He nodded and dealt me a ten of hearts, himself a five of spades.

"Pair of fives," he said, and he dealt me a queen of hearts.

His next card was a four of hearts. Mine, a ten of clubs.

"Pair of tens," he said. "This is getting interesting."

His next card was a nine of hearts.

"Your tens beat my fives. Sure you don't want to bet a little?"

"I'm sure."

He dealt me the seventh card, a deuce of diamonds.

"Looks like you have me, Ruth. Only one last chance for Mr. Streker."

He last card, which he turned over with a flourish, was a five of diamonds. He looked up, smiling.

"Three fives takes your two tens. I believe you owe me some money."

I had the money in the pocket of my dress, along with the message to Danny. But when I tried to reach for it, my arm had turned to stone.

"Two out of three." I couldn't believe I was even saying it.

His smile widened, showing his jack-o-lantern teeth.

"You really know how to brighten up a dying man's life, Ruth."

"Deal the cards, Mr. Streker," I said.

# Tusks

At their twentieth high school reunion, held at the Holiday Inn in Roscoe, Tennessee, Vic Braxton invited Tim Driscoll to go boar hunting with him the following Saturday, and Tim agreed. It seemed like a fine idea at the time. He pictured himself and Vic sitting under a tree somewhere way up in the Smokies, listening to the baying hounds and reminiscing of the days when gas was thirty-two cents a gallon and virgins were as plentiful as pigeons.

Picturing the hunting trip the way he did, Tim was surprised by his wife Phyllis's vehement reaction against it when he mentioned it to her a few evenings later at dinner.

"Hunting? With Vic Braxton? Are you having some kind of midlife crisis?"

"Give me a break, Phyllis."

"You don't even own a gun."

"I'm sure Vic has an extra one."

What are you hunting, Daddy?" asked Tim's daughter, Sue Ellen.

"Boars."

"Those big ugly things with long tusks?"

"That's right."

Sue Ellen rolled her eyes. Although barely fourteen, she was already wearing lipstick and painting her eyelids purple. Recently, Tim had overheard her talking on the phone to one of her girlfriends about sex slaves and orgies, both subjects she had learned about from TV. When he had mentioned this to Phyllis, she seemed unconcerned. "What are you going to do," she asked, "take the TV away from her? You want to turn her into a social misfit?"

Phyllis had been his high school sweetheart, and Tim still loved her after sixteen years of marriage. Lately, however, he had been having these spells where he would look at her and see a stranger. It was as if all the things they had experienced together had been obliterated and she was somebody he had never seen before—sitting in a doctor's office or a train station. Tim found this feeling deeply disturbing. It made him wonder if he was losing his mind.

Early Saturday morning, Tim was waiting for Vic on his front porch when Vic pulled into the driveway in a pickup truck. Vic's cousin, Ed Horner, was with him. Tim had Phyllis's fanny pack around his waist; the pack contained sandwiches, a granola bar, insect repellent, and a compass. He also had a thermos of coffee and a canteen of Gatorade. Vic had told him to bring his supplies in the fanny pack, explaining that a knapsack would "be murder in the slicks." Slicks were the dense thickets of rhododendron.

Tim sat in the middle between Vic and Ed. The boar hounds were in cages in the back. Vic drove up into the Smokies while Hank Williams Jr. sang about rowdy nights and lost love on the tape player. They drank coffee and watched the sky turn light.

"Hunting razorbacks is a pure thrill, Tim," Vic said, "especially the way me and Ed hunt 'em. We don't shoot 'em with a rifle. That's the chickenshit way to hunt. We get right down in the dirt and slicks and fight it out with 'em, using one of the most primitive and basic weapons there is—the hunting spear. "

"You don't use a gun?" Tim asked.

"Hell, no. That would take most of the fun out of it. Tell him, Ed. Ain't boar hunting with a spear the biggest thrill you've ever experienced?"

"Nothing else like it," Ed said.

"A boar has got heart," Vic said. "He's meaner than a pit bull when you get him cornered, and he'll fight like one, too. If you don't believe me, look at this." Vic pulled up his shirt to show Tim a star-shaped scar on his stomach. "Old boar did that to me last summer. I was going to spear him and slipped in the mud, and he took a chunk out of me."

"That was one mean boar," Ed said. "He'd already tore up Pearly and Toot."

"Pearly ain't never been right since that boar got ahold to him." Vic held up his index finger, his thumb at the base. "Critter had tusks that long."

"What happened to the boar?" Tim asked. "Did he get away?"

"We fought that rascal all over the ridge," Vic said. "I got my spear in him three times, and Ed stabbed him twice. When he finally went down, I liked to have cried I was so happy."

"One got ahold to me last year, too," Ed said. "Up on Devil's Mountain." Ed pulled up his pants to show Tim a six-inch scar on his calf.

"Do you think we'll get one today?" Tim was feeling nauseated, but he thought maybe it was from going around the mountain curves.

"I believe we will," Ed said. "We got skunked the last two times out, and three is a lucky number."

"My third marriage sure didn't turn out so good," Vic said.

"Why is that, Vic?" Tim asked.

"We never loved each other. I thought what I felt was love but it turned out to be just another case of rutting fever."

Tim admired Vic's down-to-earth way of looking at things. Last week he had seen a talk show on TV that focused on divorced couples discussing their marital problems. The participants had used phrases like "different values," "conflicting career paths," and "a breakdown in communication." He wondered how Vic would sound on a show like that: *Dr. Phil, our main problem was we weren't in love. It was just another case of rutting fever.*

Vic drove through a valley deep in McSwain County, on the Tennessee-Carolina line. Turning off the paved road, he followed a dirt road through a pasture. At the end of the road, Vic pulled off onto the side, and they got out. Tim could hear the dogs barking in the back.

After they urinated in the road, Vic got the spears out of the truck bed. They were about seven feet long, with triangular-shaped metal heads.

"Here's your weapon," he said, handing Tim a spear. "It's got a razor-sharp edge, so be careful. You need to get the feel of it before you use it. I wouldn't try throwing it at a boar, since that takes practice. These throw good, but if you don't bring him down on that first throw, you're without a weapon after that, and that gives your boar a right smart advantage. Best thing to do is get in close and stab him with it."

"Any particular place I should aim for?" Tim asked, hefting the spear.

"I just spear him wherever I can. Ain't got time to do much aiming in a boar fight." Vic got out a notebook and pen and began drawing in it. "I want to show you where we are in case we get separated."

"There much chance of that?" Tim tried to sound nonchalant.

"Not that much. This is just to orient you to the terrain we'll be operating in."

At the top of the page Vic drew a design that indicated north, south, east, and west. Then he drew three rounded shapes about an inch apart to indicate the three mountains they would be hunting on: Poke, Devil's Mountain, and Big Rock Mountain in Carolina if the dogs ran that far.

Putting the paper in his pocket, Tim picked up the spear, which he had leaned against the side of the truck, and took a couple of practice jabs with it.

While Ed got their fanny packs and canteens out of the back, Vic opened the cages and let the dogs out. Tim counted seven, all lean and sinewy and mud-brown. The dogs ran around in circles, sniffing the air, the ground, the wet places the men had left; then they took off across the field, disappearing into a stand of hardwoods.

Tim, Vic, and Ed started across the field at a brisk pace. At the end of the field they climbed a steep ridge, following a path that ran around the mountain. Tim could hear the dogs yelping and barking farther up the ridge.

Awhile later, they left the path and moved up through a laurel thicket, ablaze with pink rhododendron.

"It gets a little rough here," Vic said. "You need to go through this shit low, like a bear. If you get lost, best thing to do is keep low and get out at the next clear place. It's also important to stay calm. Many a poor soul has lost his mind in a mountain slick. Also, you got to watch out for bear in here."

"What do I do if I see one?" Tim was already breathing hard.

"Run," Vic said.

"I'll have to stop first and empty out my britches," Tim said, and Ed and Vic laughed.

At midmorning they stopped to rest in a hollow by a stream. Tim ate one of his sandwiches, then lay back in a bed of ferns. A ray of sunlight fell through the leaves, painting a golden swath on the water. He could no longer hear the dogs, only the murmur of the stream and the wind rustling the leaves overhead.

"Tim, you know what boars like to eat?" Vic asked.

"Roots and things?"

"They eat roots and berries. But they also like copperheads and rattlers."

"Is that right?"

"Ain't nothing they love better than a snake. Poison don't faze 'em."

Tim picked up his spear and hefted it in his hand. Since this was his first trip out he thought maybe he should just throw the spear at a boar and let Vic and Ed finish it off. It just made good sense to watch how they did it first before attempting a close-quarters fight with a beast that ate rattlesnakes for breakfast.

They ate lunch on the western slope of Poke Mountain, overlooking a valley of hardwood and pine. West of the valley was Devil's Mountain, the eastern slopes abloom with purple laurel. In the distance more mountains lay beneath a lavender haze. Above the haze the sky was a blue sea strewn with whitecap clouds.

Tim sat on a fallen tree and ate his ham-and-cheese sandwiches, washing them down with Gatorade. His legs ached, and he was soaked with sweat. He could hear the hounds barking and howling in the distance. They had found several boar trails, but Vic said they were all cold.

"Sure is pretty up here," Tim said.

"We're in God's pocket now," Vic said.

"Listen," Ed said. "Sounds like they've got a hot trail."

"They're just fussing," Vic said.

The baying rose, subsided, rose, then grew faint again.

"Cold trail," Vic said, taking a bite out of a candy bar.

Tim was thinking about all of the animals he had seen so far that morning: raccoons, rabbits, a fox, crows, an eagle, a woodpecker, and an opossum. These mountains were full of furry, feathery creatures that knew he was there and were afraid of him. Tim was amazed that they were able to survive with no help at all from man, not even garbage cans to forage in.

"I saw some bear tracks up the ridge a ways," Vic said. "Looked like Three Toes."

"I saw those tracks, too," Ed said. "I was hoping Three Toes had made it through last season."

"Who's Three Toes?" Tim asked.

"An old black bear," Vic said. "Been up in these hills for years. They call him Three Toes cause he lost part of his foot in a trap."

"He's been mighty lucky so far, all the hunters coming up here with rifles," Ed said.

"They'll get him, sooner or later," Vic said. "Assholes."

Tim put his hand back behind the log, and impaled his index finger on a thorn. He squeezed it and watched a drop of blood come out. He raised his finger to his tongue. He could feel his heart beating, pushing the blood through his veins.

Halfway up the side of one of the mountains, he sat beneath an outcropping of gray rock, rubbing a cramp out of his leg. His feet were blistered, and his legs ached. He was sweaty, winded, and lost. It worried him that if he got separated from Vic and Ed, all he had to guide him back to the truck was a crude map on a sheet of notebook paper. Vic and Ed called the mountains by name, but one mountain just looked like the next one to him. He regretted letting Vic Braxton talk him into such an insane idea as this hunt;

it was clear he just wasn't in shape for it. He should have worked up to it by jogging or working out at the spa.

He heard the dogs howling nearby, but there was a new, more frantic energy in their cries: their chorus set his heart to racing and made him forget his pain. Using the spear as a walking stick, he went along the slope. He came to another laurel thicket and crawled under the thick leaves, through air perfumed by the pink blossoms. "Vic!" he called. "Vic, Where are you?" He was surrounded by thin, twisted trunks and forked branches covered with red bark. Overhead, a thick, low canopy of leathery leaves. He felt a tightness in his chest. What if he came eyeball to eyeball with a snake?

It sounded like the dogs were above him, to the right. He tried to head in that direction, but it was slow going through the thicket. He wondered what all was in this soil: insect dung no doubt, bits of digested seeds that had passed through the rear ends of birds, decomposed fur and feathers, the bones of hikers who had lost their way and died of snakebite, exposure, or malnutrition. Tim imagined the lost hikers had gone mad before they died, thinking the circling buzzards were helicopters coming to their rescue.

There was a commotion nearby, a din of howling and barking. Someone shouted, but he couldn't tell if it was Vic or Ed.

He broke through the laurel, and about a hundred yards down the slope he saw the hounds, baying and lunging into another laurel thicket. Interspersed with the baying hounds was another sound, a hacking grunt.

He went down the slope, gripping the spear. Where were Vic and Ed? If he could just get a look at the damn thing, he thought he'd feel less afraid. Not seeing it preyed on his mind, made his legs weak.

A shrill howling arose from the slick. Then a welter of growling, snarling and that coughing grunt that raised chill bumps on his arms. The whole thicket was shaking, as if blown by a strong wind. What should he do?

He decided to stay where he was. Damned if he wanted to crawl into a laurel thicket and risk getting attacked by something he hadn't even seen yet.

Suddenly, a section of the laurel thicket jiggled, as if stirred by a gust of wind, and a black beast shot out, bellowing and grunting. It was followed by dogs, and, a split second later, Vic.

Surrounded by dogs, the boar whirled around and lunged at them. Howling and barking, the dogs feinted, backed off, and attacked the boar from the rear. One of the dogs locked its jaws onto the boar's back leg, and they went around and around in a blur of motion. Tim stood there holding the spear, not knowing to do. He saw Vic's spear flash and heard the boar bellow.

Tim ran right into the melee, but before he could take aim at the boar, he lost his footing and suddenly he was on his back, looking at the cloud-strewn sky. He sat up and saw the boar coming toward him. With its long snout, black bristling head and bloody tusks, it looked like something out of the deepest pits of hell. The boar hit him before he could stand, knocking his legs out from under him. He smelled its foul musk and felt a burning pain in his thigh. He heard the dogs howling in his ears as they ran over him.

He sat up and saw the boar running up the slope, trailed by the dogs and Vic.

Tim stood up on wobbly legs. His pants were torn. He touched his thigh and his fingers came away bloody.

On up the slope the boar had one of the dogs down.

Ed burst out of the slick and headed up the hill.

Tim ran after him. Something flashed in his brain, and he felt a force move through him. He ran in close to the boar, pushing Ed out of the way in his frenzy, and plunged the spear into the boar's side. They went around and around, the boar grunting and bellowing, trying to bite the dogs. Tim felt as if he had impaled some huge muscle, the heart of the wilderness. The boar spun around and went for Ed, nearly jerking the spear out of Tim's hands. Ed tried to spear him but missed.

Vic came up suddenly from the side and speared the boar in the neck.

The boar went for Vic and then Tim, but he kept it away with the spear. He forced the spear deeper and deeper into its side, and suddenly the animal was down, grunting and bellowing, the dogs swarming over it, the boar still slashing at them with its tusks.

A guttural howl rose above the din. Tim was astonished to realize the sound was coming from him.

Riding down the mountain that night, they drank whiskey out of Dixie cups and talked about the hunt.

Vic said the boar was not only one of the biggest he had ever seen but that it had also put up one of the best fights. The boar was on the truck bed now, wrapped in a tarpaulin. Vic had cut off its head with a hacksaw and put the head in a gunnysack, to be mounted later by a taxidermist.

Vic had medicated and bandaged the gash in Tim's thigh. Both Vic and Ed said he was lucky that the cut wasn't that deep into the muscle. Vic told him the boar had "just opened up the meat a little." Still the gash had hurt until he had started drinking the whiskey. He couldn't feel it much now.

"That boar put up a great fight," Ed said. "Look what he did to Midnight."

Midnight, one of the dogs, had been cut up pretty bad by the boar. Vic had sewn up the dog's wounds with a needle and thread. Although he said Midnight would probably survive, he wasn't sure whether he would ever be able to fight again.

"Midnight loves to fight razorbacks," Vic said. "Be a crying shame if he can't hunt again."

"He's about the best catch dog we got," Ed said.

"Catch dog?" Tim asked.

"There's two basic kinds of hog dogs. Chase dogs run 'em. Catch dogs take over when the fighting starts."

"I like dogs," Tim said. He had wanted to get one once, but Phyllis had vetoed the idea. "A dog is nothing but trouble," she had said. "They slobber all over you and they have bad breath."

"Ain't no better friend than a good dog," Vic said. "He'll still love you when everyone else has left you high and dry."

"Love you when you stink, love you when you ugly," Ed said. "You can count on that."

When they pulled into Tim's driveway, the house was dark, but Phyllis had left the porch light on.

"I really appreciate you all letting me come with you," Tim said.

"Our pleasure," Vic said. "You look after that leg now."

Tim was limping up to his house when he heard Vic call his name. Vic was getting something out of the back of the truck: the sack containing the boar's head.

"Me and Ed decided to give you this trophy."

Tim tried to decline, but Vic insisted. "Take it, Tim. You earned it."

"What should I do with it?"

"Put it in the freezer until you can take it to the taxidermist. I'll call you tomorrow and give you his name and address."

Tim thanked Vic and limped into the house, carrying the boar's head. His wound throbbed, his muscles ached, his feet hurt, and his hands were raw and lacerated from thorns and rocks.

He found a note from Phyllis on the dining room table, telling him his supper was in the fridge. He set the bag on the kitchen floor, took off the fanny pack, and got out his supper: Kentucky Fried chicken, potato salad, and slaw. He got out beer, too, and sat down at the kitchen counter to eat.

After he finished eating he opened the freezer compartment and cleared out a space for the boar's head. He lifted the boar's massive head out of the sack and set it down in the freezer. Even in death, the boar's head looked awesome. Its jet black eyes seemed to glitter with menace, its tusks still had specks of dried blood on them. Tim shivered as he remembered the thing coming after him. He closed the freezer and refrigerator door and put the burlap sack under the sink. He cleaned up the blood that had dripped from the head with a paper towel.

He hadn't really wanted the boar's head: he had only accepted it to keep from hurting Vic's feelings. He could see he had a problem on his hands since Phyllis would never allow him to display it in their house. He couldn't put it in his law office, either; it would turn off too many of his clients.

I'll figure out what to do about it later, he thought.

He got another beer out of the refrigerator, then climbed the stairs to the second floor. In the hall bathroom he set the beer bottle on the sink, took off his clothes, and sat on the side of the tub looking at his thigh; the bandage was soaked with blood. He guessed he had torn the cut open moving around. He took off the bandage to look at the wound. It was about four inches long. He got up, looking for a washcloth to wipe the blood off his leg. He couldn't find one, so he got a towel off the rack by the sink. Sitting down again he knocked the beer bottle onto the floor. He was trying to wipe up the floor with the towel when Phyllis appeared in the doorway.

"Oh, my God, Tim!"

"It's all right, honey. It's just a scratch."

"You're bleeding on the floor!"

"I'll clean it up."

"What's wrong with you?" Phyllis cried. "What happened to the man I married?"

Tim knew he should try to console her, but at that moment he had another one of those spells when his wife seemed to be a stranger. Sue Ellen appeared beside her, and the two of them stared at him like he was an ax murderer. "Daddy, are you drunk?"

Tim, who now felt as bestial and ugly as the head in the freezer, could think of nothing to say in his own defense. He looked down at his wound. This is going to make a fine scar, he thought. He gazed up at his wife and daughter, trying to think of a way to share his pleasure at having realized he would now have a scar like Vic and Ed.

"I want a dog," he heard himself say. His request burst suddenly out of some deep, secret place—a mountain cave hidden by a laurel thicket. "Do you hear me? I want a goddamned dog!"

# Starlene's Baby

The light is on in Starlene's living room when I drive by her house at three A.M., on the way out to the highway to pick up my papers at the Quik-Stop. I know she is sitting up with the baby. When I drive back by the house again the sun is a bloody egg over the pines, and J.J.'s truck is gone. He's perched in a tree somewhere, hoping to get a deer in his sights. Starlene will be up now, too, fixing breakfast for Rebecca and John, Jr., to get them off to school, one of them holding that baby, poor little honey. Eleven months old and can't even hold its head up, can't even say "ma-ma" or "da-da." But he can flat raise Cain if someone ain't holding him. He's got to be held every minute of each day and night. They done spoilt that baby which Starlene never should have had. They all take turns holding him, but it's Starlene who has to sit up with him most of the night. I reckon she has got used to sleeping sitting up.

I pull off the dirt road into our driveway, park my Plymouth in front of our trailer. Inside, my old man is still snoring in the recliner where he fell asleep last night watching TV. I used to get him up and make him come sleep in the bed, but no more. Let him sleep where he's of a mind to, is the way I look at it now. How he can watch that TV ten, twelve hours a day is beyond me. Long as he's got cigarettes and Pepsis he'll sit there, getting up only to go to the bathroom. He eats breakfast and lunch in front of the TV, too, on a tray, and he'd eat supper there, too, if I'd let him, but I draw the line at that. He don't sit with me at suppertime, he don't eat, at least not something I've fixed for him.

He's been like that ever since he retired from the county hospital, where he worked in maintenance. Lloyd ain't never had much ambition.

In the kitchen sink I wash the newsprint off my hands. I put on a pot of coffee and fix myself some ham and eggs. Soon I hear the old man stirring.

I hear the toilet flush, and then he shuffles into the kitchen, red-eyed, two gray tufts of hair sticking up on each side of his head. He don't look happy.

"Them pintos I eat last night give me gas," he says, lighting a cigarette.

"Don't git around me, then."

He pours himself a cup of coffee and goes on into the living room. Turning on the TV with the remote control, he begins flipping through the channels.

I get up and go into the room.

"Want me to fix you a bite to eat?"

Lloyd don't answer, which means No. He is frowning at the TV, where a man is talking about an earthquake out in California. I see a buckled highway, a collapsed bridge.

"Them people ain't been paying the preacher," the old man says.

"You can't buy salvation," I tell him. He sends money every month to them TV preachers, and they send him two, three letters a week begging for more. If he didn't give me his check every month I swear he'd send it all to them, leaving me to keep him in cigarettes and Pepsis and pay all the bills, too.

"Most of them preachers is just after money," I tell him, but he don't listen to me.

It's a pity to see all those stamps and letters go to waste. If those TV preachers is so close to God, how come don't none of them know the old man can't read?

I wake up and hear the TV going. I use the john and go down the hall, see the old man asleep in the chair, the ashtray on the end table full of cigarette butts.

I sit at the table and check my route books to see who has paid and who ain't, and I make out new bills for the ones who still owe. After awhile I got to get out of the house so I drive down the road to see Starlene and her baby.

She's forty-three and too old to have a baby. After she found out, the doctors did some tests and told her it won't going to be right. They wanted

her to get rid of it, but she wouldn't listen. "I'm going to have my baby," she said, even though a baby was the last thing she needed, especially one that won't right. They could barely make out as it was, and after that baby came they lost the money she brought in cleaning houses and running my route for me when I was sick or just needed a day off. Now all they got coming in is J.J.'s disability check. I reckon they'd starve if it won't for their garden and the meat and fish J.J. brings home. He used to drive a truck, but he got hurt in a wreck a few years ago and ain't hit a lick of work since then. Claims to have a bad back, but any man who can climb trees and clean deer ain't in that bad a shape, you ask me.

Their house is a mile up the road from us, on the left going toward the highway. They got four rooms and a roof that leaks when it rains. Ain't hardly enough room for her and J.J., let alone the three others.

I park in the driveway and walk up the steps to the screen door. She sees me and hollers for me to come in.

She is sitting on the sofa in the living room, holding the baby, waiting for J.J. to come back from hunting I reckon, so she can do some chores. Rebecca and Buddy are in school.

"Hey, Vera Mae," she says. She is skinny everywhere but her belly. Back when she was working it was flat as a fritter. She's a worker, Starlene is. Ain't nothing slack about her. She'll run my route in two hours and forty minutes and never miss a customer.

"I just stopped by to see how you're doing," I say.

"Stomach's been giving me trouble," she says, laying a hand on her belly.

"Something's been going around. Lloyd had the runs all last week." I sit beside her on the couch and smile at the poor little thing. He is huge for eleven months, and his head is the biggest thing about him. You can tell there's something wrong. His forehead bulges out like a baby Frankenstein. Eyes in nervous orbit like two blue moons.

"Want to hold him?" Starlene asks.

"Give him here." I hold out my hands and take him from her. He is all warm and sweet smelling. "You are getting heavy."

"He don't do nothing but eat," Starlene says.

He quivers in my arms, wiggling his stubby fingers.

"It's just old Vera Mae. I ain't going to take you away from your mama."

"I got to do a load of wash," she says, but she just sits there, looking at him. His hair is fine and yellow like corn silk and his skin soft and ruddy and blue-veined. Looking at just those two things you can imagine the perfect picture Starlene would have dreamed.

"Ain't you something?" I make a sound like a motor against his soft neck. He squeals.

"You like that? You like that, little feller?" I do it again.

"He's a mess," Starlene says.

"I wish you'd bring him down to see the old man. This baby is about the only thing that will get him to switch off the TV."

"I'll be by before long."

"Gubagubaguba," I say to the baby. He squeals again. He is just a dead weight in my arms, and him growing fast as a watermelon in July.

"Can you hold him while I put a load of clothes in the washer?" Starlene asks.

"Sure."

She goes back through the kitchen to the back porch, where her washing machine is. I hold him up with his fat legs falling down between mine, the back of his head resting against my chest.

"Clap handies," I say, clapping his hands together. "Patty cake, patty cake, baker's man, bake me a cake as fast as you can."

I shut my eyes tight and get a big smell of him. "Mmmmmm," I tell him. "You smell good enough to eat."

Starlene comes back in. "You got time for me to pick some snap beans and 'maters?"

"I ain't in no hurry."

"I won't be long."

"We'll just come outside with you." Holding him snug against my chest I follow her through the kitchen, which smells of baby poop from the diaper pail in the corner, out to the back porch, past the thug-thug-thug of the old washing machine rocking next to the freezer, and down the steps to the back yard. I sit in a cane chair by the steps, the baby in my lap, while Starlene walks through the rows picking snap beans, putting them into a paper bag. A breeze stirs up, rippling the clothes hanging on the line strung between a post and the chinaberry tree at the end of the garden.

"I'm glad you come by," Starlene calls out. She is bent over so I can see the outline of her panties under her thin cotton pants. "When J.J.'s gone and the young'uns are at school, ain't no one to hold him but me. I can't get nothing done."

You shouldn't have spoilt this baby, Starlene, I want to say, but I hold my tongue.

"I'm picking you a mess of beans," she says.

"That's all right." I don't want to take any of her food. "We got plenty."

"How 'bout some tomatoes?"

"Got plenty of them, too," I lie.

A robin swoops down to light on the clothesline post.

"Look, look," I tell the baby. And I hold him up, supporting his neck with my hand, aiming him toward the bird. "See the pretty bird?"

I turn him around and lay him down backwards in my lap so the back of his head is resting on my knees. His eyes, blue and empty as the sky, make lazy circles in his plump face.

"Gubagubaguba," I say, and I tickle his stomach, trying to get him to laugh.

That afternoon when I drive by their house J.J. has a doe hanging by her hind legs from the limb of the chinaberry tree out back. He is pulling her insides out into a washtub. He waves his bloody hand at me, but I pretend I don't see him. I ain't got much use for J.J. and he knows it.

At least he could get her pregnant, I think, which is more than I can say for Lloyd. Won't my fault, the doctor said, although I had some scarring in my tubes. The main problem was Lloyd. His seed was bad.

But we still kept trying. All those years. Hoping we might get lucky.

It was just as well, I tell myself now. We could have had one like Starlene's baby—a poor little honey that can't grab ahold to your finger, can't even raise his head to see a bird. What kind of life would that be?

I am near the end of my route when a rabbit runs under my wheels.

I stop the car, get out my flashlight, and walk back to where it lays in the road, legs stretched like it is still running.

Her belly is full with babies that won't ever see the light of day.

I push her off the road with my foot and go back to the car. I have a headache, and my knees are hurting. Times like this I think about giving my paper route up. I'm sixty-four, and I been running it five years now. That's about four years too many, but the money is good considering the actual time you put in, and I don't have to put up with much crap from anyone. That's the worse part of most jobs, dealing with other people. As long as I do my job right, I don't get any complaints. We're supposed to get the papers out by 6:30, but I'm usually done by 6:00. This job has its downsides. The hours are sliced out of the night when a normal person is sleeping, and it's seven days a week, three hundred and sixty-five days a year. But ain't no one around to give you any lip, and that's what I like about it. About the only thing out this time of night is deer and rabbits, and they ain't going to argue with you or give you any grief.

Animals ain't got souls, I think, as I sail the papers over the roof of the Plymouth. But every misfit human has got one, and every one made in His own image. I try to see the beauty in this, but sometimes it's hard to do. I can't understand why He would make a baby cursed in its mama's womb.

First Saturday in October Starlene comes to visit, bringing the baby with her. He is cute as a bug's ear in his little sailor's suit. I wonder where she got the money to buy him that.

The old man switches off the TV when they come in. Starlene sets the baby in his lap.

"My, ain't you a handsome little feller," he says, bouncing the baby on his knee. "You been eating pretty good, ain't you? Yes, siree, I can see you ain't been missing no meals."

The baby squeals, flashing his red gums.

"He likes you, Lloyd," Starlene says.

"Babies always liked Lloyd," I say. "Babies and dogs."

"Dogs is scared of J.J.," Starlene says.

"You're a little hoss," Lloyd says.

"Want some Kool-Aid, Starlene?" She don't drink coffee since she's still nursing.

"OK."

She follows me to the kitchen and sits at the table while I get the Kool-Aid out of the fridge.

"I went to the doctor yesterday," she says. "He says I got a tumor."

"Where is it?"

"My right ovary. He says they need to operate."

"My sister-in-law had that operation, and she got all right."

"What would happen to him if I died?"

"You ain't going to die," I tell her.

"I will sooner or later, and then who will take care of him?"

"He's got J.J. and Rebecca and John, Jr."

"He'd be lost without me." Tears shine in her eyes.

I sit down beside her, take her hand in mine. In the next room I hear Lloyd talking to the baby. "Everything will be all right, Starlene."

She wipes her eyes with her fist.

"Lloyd and me will look after him while you are in the hospital."

"But what if I don't come home, Vera?"

"You'll come home, honey."

She wipes her eyes again with her fist.

"I ain't never loved no one like I love him," she says.

Every morning while Starlene is in the hospital, I stop at her house and pick up the baby on the way home from my route. He stays with me and Lloyd until around four o'clock when Rebecca or Buddy come to pick him up. I can tell by their puffy, red eyes they are the ones sitting up with him.

While the baby is with us, Lloyd don't even turn the TV on. We take turns holding him, changing his diapers, talking to him. He is some trouble since his face turns red and his siren goes off if you set him down more than a minute. But even so, we get so we hate to see them coming to pick him up.

Starlene calls every day, wanting to know how he is.

"Put the receiver up to his ear so he can hear my voice," she says, and I put the phone up to his ear.

"Hey, honey," I hear her say through the phone. "It's Mama. I'm coming home soon."

The trees is stark and black in the gray light. Mornings when I go out to my car, my knees and hips ache in the biting cold. This is my last winter doing this, I tell myself. But I remember I said the same thing last winter, and the one before that, too.

Every morning when I drive by Starlene's house, the light is on in the living room where she is trying to sleep sitting up, the baby in her arms. Her belly is almost flat now, and when I visit her she don't talk about dying anymore. I wonder how they can keep on like that, with only J.J.'s income and her holding him all the time. And what if something did happen to her? J.J. wouldn't hardly be able to take care of him, and Rebecca and Buddy would have their own lives to live. He'd most likely end up in an asylum somewhere where no one would ever hold him. He could scream his head off for all they'd care. I feel sorry for her, but that burden is her own fault.

"I worry about Starlene," I tell Lloyd one night. "How's she gonna keep taking care of that baby?"

"She can give him to us," he says.

"That's the last thing we need."

I am nursing Starlene's baby. I am full of milk, so full my breasts hurt. I press him against me and smell his clean, sweet baby smell. When he finishes, my breasts feel better and his belly is tight and hard with my milk.

The alarm goes off, and I get up and put on my clothes in the dark. My knees is stiff. My back hurts. I am getting too old to be doing this.

It's snowing outside. I am glad I got snow tires put on the car. Folks got to have their papers in the morning; they don't care if there's snow on the ground or not.

I drive the winding road, thinking about that dream. A buck leaps into the road ahead. I slam on the brakes, the car skidding into a ditch. I put it in reverse and gun it until I smell rubber burning.

Lord, I think. Lloyd's car is in the shop, and I have got to get my papers delivered.

I get out and walk through the snow to Starlene's house. Everything is still and white and lovely, the snow falling like big chips of soap. I knock on the door and she answers in her pajamas, hugging that baby to her chest, him all wrapped in a blue blanket, the room smelling of burning kerosene from the heater on the floor.

"Starlene, I sure hate to bother you, honey, but I run in a ditch, and I got to get them durn newspapers delivered. Reckon you could wake up J.J. and get him to pull me out with his truck?"

"Come on in."

I stomp the snow off my boots and go in. She gives me the baby to hold while she goes to wake up J.J. Lord, how I hate to ask that man for help.

I stand there by the door, holding the baby tight against my coat, looking down at his ruddy face, his long lashes, his bud-like mouth that is busy working on his thumb. Suddenly, I don't want to give him back to her. God forgive me for what I want to do, run with him before she comes back, into the snowy night, and keep on running until I find someplace to hide, someplace far away where Starlene and J.J. could never find us. I lift him to my face, smelling his skin. "Mmm, you smell good as hot biscuits," I say. "Starlene better come quick before I eat you up."

# The Driver

I'm approaching the intersection of 13th and Hays Boulevard when this woman in a camouflage jacket jabs something hard into my back and tells me to turn right on Hays. I can see her in the curved overhead mirror. Flinty eyes set close together, a broad nose for a white woman, a swollen face like someone who eats too much salt. On the seat beside her there is a knapsack, a pile of newspapers. I turn right and say, "You want the money, you can have it."

"Shut up," she says.

In the opposite lane I see a police car. My eyes linger on it as it passes, and I feel an increase in the pressure against my kidney. I glance in the mirror at the other passengers. Across the aisle on the front seats, there are two white boys about eighteen or nineteen, with moussed hair and skinny faces. Behind them two empty seats and then a middle-aged white woman with red hair. Immediately behind the gunwoman's seat, there is a sister in a nurse's uniform. Behind her, a silver-haired man in a coat and tie, and behind him, a young brother in shades and a blue smock like food service workers wear. The others, sitting in the back, are elderly people mostly, on their way to their banks to cash their Social Security checks.

The passengers are looking around now. They can tell something is wrong. One of the white boys says, "Excuse me, sir. Aren't we supposed to be going downtown?"

The pressure increases against my kidney. I don't say a word. I picture my son's face, staring up at me from his bed at night. Abe is three and won't go to sleep until I come in and kiss him good night.

When I stop at a red light, the woman jumps up and whips a long-barreled revolver out from under her jacket. She has another one aimed at my head. "I'm taking over this bus!" she announces. "We're going for a little ride, and everyone is gonna do just like I say, including mister driver here. Any questions?"

There is a murmur of voices. The two boys are embracing, cheeks pressed together like they are doing a tango.

The silver-haired man raises a trembling hand. "Excuse me," he says, "but I've got a doctor's appointment. For my heart."

"Tough shit, old-timer."

She sits down, taps me on the shoulder with the barrel. "Let's go, driver. You got a green light."

I shift into first and ease out the clutch, heading south on Hays Boulevard. She asks me if I know where Washington Street is, and I tell her yes.

"I want you to turn right on Washington."

My route plan calls for me to go straight on 13th, all the way downtown. I think about the people waiting for me to come, thinking I am late. My supervisor will be aggravated when he finds out I'm not doing my route. He is a fat white man with eyes set close together, like this woman with the gun. When he gets mad his eyes bug out, and he shakes his head so hard the fat jiggles on his jaws.

"Are you gonna kill us?" one of the boys asks.

"Hush," the other one says, slapping him on the back of the head. "For Christsakes!"

As I turn right on Washington I remember a conversation my wife, Sonya, and I had last month about my life insurance. I've got fifty thousand on me now; they take the premium out of my paycheck. I told her I could get fifty more for forty a month, and I asked her if I should do it. "I don't know, honey," she said, frowning. "Do we have to talk about it now?" That's Sonya. She doesn't like to admit the possibility of bad things happening. I kept thinking about the things I could buy for Abe with the forty a month— clothes, toys, books. Or we could just put it in a savings account for his college. I ended up putting the issue on a back burner, and now I am thinking what a bad move that was.

"Miss. Excuse me. Miss. "

"You talking to me?" the gunwoman asks, turning to look at the red-haired woman.

"This man isn't well."

In the mirror I see the top of the old man's head. He is resting his forehead against the seat.

"No wonder, all the shit they're putting in the air. I don't feel so fucking good myself. How about minding your own business?"

I consider trying to jump her, grab her gun. But that would be hard since I'm driving the bus. I might be able to get one of them. Problem is, she could shoot me with the other one.

I think of Sonya raising Abe alone. Picture him looking up at her at night and asking for me. "Where's my daddy? I want my daddy." We still owe seventy-some thousand on our house, eight thousand on the Mercury, five hundred to Sears for the washer and dryer. That fifty grand wouldn't go very far.

Before I went to work for the city, I drove a Yellow Cab. Sonya talked me into applying for this job. "It's safer," she said. "There's all kinds of crazies walking the streets today, and you're a sitting duck in a cab. People kill cab drivers all the time. Cab drivers and 7-Eleven clerks. But who ever heard of a bus driver getting shot?"

I know of two, right here in our city. Last year, a drunk shot Monk Riley through the lungs after Monk tried to put him off the bus. Year before that a bullet hit Alma Harris in the temple. She slumped over the wheel, and the bus hit a telephone pole. Police never caught the shooter. Could have been some gangbanger messing around. I've seen them down on 14th Street, spinning their pistols on their fingers.

Anyway, that's two bus drivers shot, one dead, and two plus one make three.

"Take the next right," she says, and that's when I get an idea of where we're going.

At the end of the street, surrounded by a twelve-foot stone wall, is Central Prison, a huge brick building so old it has four towers on its four corners. I drive up to the front gate, a steel mesh fence topped by barbed wire. There is a guard in a booth to the right of the fence.

The gunwoman points a finger at one of the boys, the one sitting by the aisle. "You—sissy britches. I want you to deliver a message for me."

"Yes, ma'am." The boy's eyes remind me of Bambi's.

"I want you to take this letter up to the warden. And tell that fucker in the booth I got a dozen hostages in here plus two .357 Magnums. I've also got plastic explosive in a Velcro lining around my belt, and it's connected by a wire to this little doohickey in my pocket so I can set it off anytime I want. All that's in the letter, but it should get you through to the warden faster."

The boy squeezes his companion's hand, then stands up.

"Okay, mister driver," she says. "Open the door and let him out."

I pull the handle, the door opens, and the boy heads up to the gate to see the warden.

She wants her man, Vince Klenner. He is in the prison, and she's going to kill everyone on the bus if she doesn't get him in two hours. I've learned this by listening to her talk to the hostage negotiator they've sent in. I can hear the police radios crackling outside. We can't see their vehicles now because she has ordered the other boy to tape newspapers over all the windows. "So a SWAT sniper can't send anything my way" is the way she put it. She told me to park the bus on the lawn in front of the prison, then handcuffed me to the steering wheel. She directed the boy to leave spaces between the papers so she can peep out. Through the windows in the front door, I can see the gate and a section of the brick building that is the color of dried blood.

The hostage negotiator calls her "Miss Fritz."

She is sitting behind me, holding a gun on the negotiator, who sits directly across her in the aisle, his feet on the floor, the other boy having been moved by her to the seat behind. The hostage negotiator, a roly-poly bald man with blue eyes, speaks to her in a voice that makes me think of something you'd pour on pancakes. By now their positions are clear. He wants to get some of the people off the bus; she wants to see Vince damn soon or people are going to start dying.

"You tell that asshole warden to get Vince out here," she says. "I wanna see him. How do I know they even got him? They could've killed him for all I know."

"No one has hurt Mr. Klenner," the negotiator says.

"How do you know that? You seen him?"

"No, but Warden Grady has assured me Mr. Klenner is fine."

"You expect me to believe that lying scumbag?"

"Miss Fritz, let's get back to the hostages. Could you at least let the sick man go? I've got to have something positive to take back to the warden, a sign of good faith on your part."

The hostage negotiator has a line of sweat above his upper lip. His head is sweating, too. He tells her if she lets the old man go he believes it will strengthen her position.

She's quiet a minute, then she orders the old man up to the front. The nurse and red-haired woman help him up. He is pale and sweating.

"Today is your lucky day," she says. "I'm gonna let you go."

"I appreciate that, Miss Fritz," the hostage negotiator says.

"Just remember I want Vince. Out here on this bus. If I don't get him, blood is gonna flow in here."

"I'm relaying your demand to the warden, Miss Fritz, but please understand there are limits on what he can do."

Miss Fritz looks at her watch. "Forty minutes. That's all the time you got."

"I'm going to do the best I can," the negotiator says, wiping his head with a handkerchief. "The absolute best I can."

There is a TV van out there. Through a crack in the newspapers on the side window I can see a woman talking into a camera.

Miss Fritz can't see the gate from her seat. I'm supposed to tell her what's going on up there. She's got the boy looking, too. He keeps his eye to a space between the newspapers.

"You tell me if you see him coming, you hear?" she says.

"Yes, ma'am."

"And let me know if you see anything suspicious, too. Else you're gonna be the first one I shoot when the shit hits the fan."

"Yonder he comes," the boy says.

When he comes back to the bus, the negotiator says he needs more time, that the warden is trying to get in touch with the governor.

"Please be patient, Miss Fritz. Lines of communication have to be opened, people have to be gotten ahold of, you have to follow the chain of command."

"What do I have to do to prove to you people that I mean business?" Miss Fritz jumps up, grabs the boy by his hair and puts the muzzle of the gun in his ear. "You want some fucking brains to take back in your handkerchief?"

Tears stream out of the boy's eyes as the hostage negotiator talks to her in that heavy sweet voice of his. I have a sick feeling as I look at this. This boy has a mama somewhere and a daddy, too. He is a part of God. What she is doing now makes me want to do something terrible to Miss Fritz, like pull out her tongue by the roots. I want to make her suffer the way she is making us suffer.

I close my eyes and hold my free hand over my ear, waiting for the shot.

But it doesn't come.

Instead, Miss Fritz decides to extend her deadline by one hour. But that's it, she says. After that, people are going to die.

The hostage negotiator is stubborn, I'll give him that. He asks if he can take some more people off the bus.

"Until I get Vince, only people you're gonna take off here will be in body bags."

After the negotiator leaves, we all sit there quietly, listening to the crackle of police radios outside the bus, the sobbing boy.

Miss Fritz cocks the hammer on one of her revolvers, then eases it back down with her thumb. "Fuck a duck," she says.


I missed my lunch break, but I'm not hungry.

I wonder if Sonya has heard about this yet, maybe from somebody at Eastside Junior High where she teaches. If she has, I can guess what's going through her mind: Jesus Christ, is it Clarence? She'll call my supervisor and find out it's me, or maybe she'll hear my name on the radio. She'll call her mother, my mother, the preacher, her friends. What will they tell little Abe?

Vince. One man in exchange for all our lives. Sure seems like a fair trade to me. I picture the warden in his office, talking to the governor on the phone.

Just do it, I think. Please. Give her Vince and let us all go home.


Miss Fritz is eating something with a wrapper and drinking from a canteen she had in the knapsack. The canteen reminds me I'm thirsty, but damned if I'm going to ask her for a drink. When she is finished eating, she gives me the wrapper, tells me to put it in the trash can.

It's a granola bar. She takes another one out of the knapsack. Catching my eye in the mirror she winks and says, "Got to keep up my energy. There's honchos out there with rifles and shotguns, and every damn fool one of 'em dreaming of being Mr. Clint Eastwood. I got to be ready for 'em if they bust in here."

I close my eyes and picture my funeral. I see people filing into my church, my closed casket down at the front surrounded by flowers. There is a special section for all the drivers, and down at the front are Sonya and Abe.

"That's my daddy," he says, looking at me in the casket. "Get up Daddy."

The negotiator hasn't come back. He's missed the deadline she set.

"That baldheaded bastard thinks he can mess with my mind," Miss Fritz says. "But he's got another thought coming. Trouble is, they ain't taking me serious. I've got to give 'em some proof, know what I mean, mister driver?"

"Why don't you give him a little more time?"

" 'Cause I ain't in the mood to be nice today." She stands up. "You back there—in the shades. Come up to the front."

The brother in the blue smock puts his hand on his chest, and she nods yes.

"Miss, you leave that young man be!" the red-haired woman shouts.

"Want me to shoot you instead?"

The brother kneels in the aisle, begins praying. I am praying too. For God to send a lightning bolt down through the bus to strike her dead, melting her face into a gooey puddle.

"Jesus sees everything you're doing," the nurse says.

"He's off getting a piece." Miss Fritz looks at her watch. "Let's get this over with."

Just then I see the negotiator coming out from the gate.

"Wait!" I say. "There he is!"

The negotiator says the governor is meeting with his advisors to decide what to do. "The governor is giving this top priority," he says. "We just need a little more time."

The red-haired woman calls out, "Mister, tell the governor he'd better hurry! She almost killed this young man back here."

The hostage negotiator says he thinks they can work something out, but it will call for patience on everyone's part. "Please stay calm, Miss Fritz. They've brought Mr. Klenner down from his cell to a special holding cell on the first floor. That's a hopeful sign."

"That's good news," Miss Fritz says, "but you tell the governor there'd better be more good news soon. Good news in the form of Vince walking out that gate, or he can start kissing these decent citizens in here goodbye."

"The governor is doing the best he can," the hostage negotiator says, wiping his head with a handkerchief. "We're all doing the best we can."

Miss Fritz agrees to extend her deadline one more hour. To 5:30.

She stands up and announces that if anyone needs to relieve themselves they can do it in the back of the bus.

Three of the old people go, two men and a woman. The men do it standing up, their backs to us. The woman just squats down and does it on the floor.

I have to go, too, but I hold it in; I feel I have to show more self-control because I am the driver. Also, I'd have to ask her to unlock the handcuffs, and I don't want to ask her for anything. I wonder if she even has the key.

The bus smells of urine.

The negotiator comes back at 5:20. He says the warden will give her Vince in exchange for all the hostages.

"That's a crock of batshit," says Miss Fritz. "Then the SWAT team can storm in here and blow our heads off. You go back and tell 'em I got to keep me some citizens. I'll give him most of these people for Vince. But I got to keep a couple for insurance."

"I'll take this on back to them," the negotiator says. "At least we're making some progress."

"I wanna see Vince. Tell them to bring him up to the front gate so I can see him."

The negotiator says he'll see what he can do.

Miss Fritz orders me and the boy to tell her when they bring someone up to the front gate.

"They've got someone out there," the boy says.

At the window in the next seat back Miss Fritz puts her eye against the window, peering out through the crack in the newspapers. "Vince, baby," she says. "We are making progress."

Stretching my neck, I can see a man in a gray prison uniform standing just beyond the fence. He is surrounded by SWAT team members dressed all in black.

The sky above the prison is the pink shade of steak cooked medium rare.

When the hostage negotiator comes back, he and Miss Fritz work out the details of the trade. It will take place on the lawn, about halfway between the bus and the prison. The negotiator will go back and explain how everything is going to work to the SWAT team and then return to the bus. Miss Fritz will allow everyone except me and the boy off the bus. At that time the SWAT team will bring Vince Klenner out. The negotiator and hostages will walk slowly toward the prison, with the exchange taking place when the two meet.

After Vince gets on the bus, Miss Fritz and Vince will be allowed to leave. Police cars following us will have to stay at least a quarter of a mile back.

While we wait for the negotiator to return, Miss Fritz handcuffs the boy to the bar on the back of the seats. She takes out a tube, and looking at herself in the overhead mirror, she applies lipstick to her mouth.

The negotiator comes back at 6:43.

"All right, folks," he says, standing at the front of the bus. "We're all going to walk off here together."

"Come up slow, single file," Miss Fritz says. "Step down in front of the bus, and then hold still until the gate opens and they come out with Vince. I'm gonna be watching from the window. Anybody make a move I don't like, I'm gonna blow your ass away."

Up at the front gate I see a man in a gray prison uniform standing between two SWAT men who wear flak jackets and helmets and carry curved, metal shields.

The hostage negotiator steps off the bus, and Miss Fritz tells the people they can leave.

"That's it," she says, looking out through a crack in the newspapers. "Slow and easy."

The two guards and Vince come down toward the bus, the SWAT men holding the shields in front of them. The shields have slits to let them see where they are going.

Vince, who is wearing handcuffs, flashes a V at the hostages as they approach.

The exchange takes place smoothly, and the negotiator, SWAT men, and hostages move off toward the gate as Vince walks down toward the bus.

"He's wearing handcuffs," says Miss Fritz. "Hairless didn't say nothing about no goddamned handcuffs."

I open the door so Vince can climb on the bus.

"Sweet thing, you are looking good!" he says, and he cuts loose with a rebel yell. His black hair is slicked back on the top and sides, with a greasy curl sticking to his forehead.

He slides into the seat behind her, and they kiss. Miss Fritz opens one eye and sees me watching in the mirror. I look away fast.

When they break apart he says, "I'd love to see that warden's face right now—the fat-assed fool."

"Forget about him. We got to get out of here."

She unlocks my handcuffs and the boy's, too, so he can take the newspapers from the front windshield. While he does this, Miss Fritz and Vince kneel in the aisle.

After he gets the newspapers down, she tells me to get going. I start up the bus, pull it across the grass to the road, which is lined with police cars. Men with guns crouch behind their cars as we pass. I count three TV vans.

She tells me to go back out to Hays, then take Terrace Avenue out to Highway 11.

I check the rearview mirror and see the cars heading out behind us in a caravan. I can hear a helicopter overhead.

Vince says, "Dora, you ever see that James Bond flick, where he shoots a chopper out of the sky with a pistol?"

Once we are on Highway 11, heading west out of the city, Vince and Dora seem to relax a little, although the police caravan has been staying about the same distance behind us, a quarter of a mile or so back. The light is fading fast. Some of the drivers have switched on their headlights.

Vince looks at the boy and says, "Ain't you a pretty thing?"

The boy jumps like he's been goosed.

As night falls, patches of fog drift across the highway. We are in the country, maybe thirty miles outside of town. South of us is the Chocawinity River. Dora has been telling me where to turn, how fast to go. She seems to have a specific destination in mind.

The fog gets thicker, and I can no longer see the headlights of the cars behind us.

"Slow down and get ready to turn right, driver."

I brake, and a minute later she tells me to turn right onto a dirt road. After I turn, she tells me to stop and open the doors. I do this, and she's out the back.

"How the hell you doing, mister driver?" Vince asks.

"Tired," I say.

"I reckon," he says.

When Dora comes back she says, "I got the chains up. Ought to slow 'em down some."

"Step on it now, driver." Vince jabs me with the gun.

The bus wasn't designed for a road this narrow. Tree limbs scrape the bus as we go. Everything is black and foggy, and I feel like the bus is out of control. When we come to a fork, Dora tells me to stay left. After we've gone about another mile, the road ends so fast I have to slam on the brakes to keep from hitting some trees.

"End of the line," she says. Keeping the gun barrel pressed against my back, she leans over and handcuffs me to the steering column. Then she stands up, puts the knapsack on her shoulders, tells me to open the door.

"I'm gonna shoot the driver," Vince says. He is standing in the aisle, holding one of her long-barreled guns.

"Ain't no reason to kill him, Vince," Dora says.

"Please don't," I say. "I've got a family—a son."

Smiling, Vince runs the gun barrel up and down my face.

"Vince, we ain't got time for that!"

"Go on, Dora. I'll catch up with you."

She climbs down off the bus. "Vince."

I am thinking about Abe now, and tears are running down my face. In the mirror I see the boy is holding his hands over his ears like the monkey that can hear no evil.

"Tears ain't nothing but salty water," Vince says. I hear him cock the revolver. "Mister driver, I been laying up there in that stinking hellhole thinking about how nice it would be to get myself some pussy. And when I'd get tired of thinking about that I'd think about the next best thing there is in the whole world. Know what that is?"

I shake my head, no. I try to say something but no words come out, just a coughing squeak.

"Killing something." He is caressing me again with the barrel. "That's right. Ain't nothing like killing to make you feel good all over. Gives you a whole new attitude. I'll never forget the first thing I killed. It was a cat. Made the mistake of scratching me one day, and I squirted lighter fluid all over it then set it afire. Cat tore around like a balloon after you let the air out. It was trying to find relief, see, but there weren't no relief. Fire made that cat look like a piece of crispy fried bacon. Mister driver, you can't imagine how happy that little incident made me feel."

I don't trust myself to speak. I am thinking of my grandmama, who died of cancer in 1981, and my uncle Trace, who got his head cut off by the Midnight Screamer after he fell into a drunken sleep on the railroad tracks.

Vince places the muzzle against my temple. "You ready to die?"

Again, I say nothing. I feel like I have already moved past this moment, past Vince, too, into some other time and place.

"I'd like to do it." Vince's voice seems to be coming from a distance. "I'd really and truly like to watch you die, but I don't believe I will, since it 'pears it would make my old lady unhappy. So this is your lucky day, mister driver. So long."

I put my head down on the wheel. I am trembling all over. I feel my crotch turning warm, the pee running down my leg into my shoe.

On Sunday, the newspaper runs a front-page story about the hijacking and jailbreak. The story explains how the governor was worried about appearing "soft on crime" if he gave up Vince, but he authorized the trade out of concern that a bus full of dead hostages would mess up his plans for reelection. Also, the SWAT team planned to follow the bus and ambush Vince and Dora after they got off. But the two outlaws escaped on a boat. Police found it fifteen miles away, abandoned near a shelter where a car had been kept.

Vince, who was serving two life terms for murder and bank robbery, is now on the FBI's Most Wanted List. Dora is, too. It grieves me that those two are still at large. They could be sitting in the car next to you at the traffic light. Or walking behind you on a dark night. They could be living in the house next door—them or people like them, who live only for the evil self.

Things have changed since I met those two. I've got a little .38 Airweight I carry while I'm on duty, although it's strictly against regulations, and Sonya worries if I'm ten minutes late getting home. Neither of us will let Abe out of our sight. I've been having some trouble getting busy with Sonya, too, but she says not to worry, that my problem will pass in time.

I spent a lot of time and energy hating Vince and Dora, imagining all the things I would do to them if I had them in my power—until I realized I was becoming more and more like them in my thoughts. That made me see how easily I, too, could have turned out bad. I could have taken a wrong turn somewhere, and instead of backtracking just continued on in the same direction, making more mistakes as I went on and finally ended up living only for my evil self. I think that's what scares me most of all.

I still see them in my dreams. Vince's flat, nasal voice slithers around in my memory like a rattler. I feel them jabbing me with their guns, see their cold killer's eyes, and wake up in a cold sweat. I keep remembering Vince asking me if I was ready to die. They say your whole life passes in front of you, but my life suddenly seemed to be a road I had already left behind. I can see my grandmama and Uncle Trace, too. They are standing in a kind of hallway, with some other people behind them. Uncle Trace is smiling. Both him and my grandmama look like they are glad to see me again. My grandmama's lips are moving like she is in an old silent movie. I shut my eyes tight, trying to make out the words.

# Disappearances

Frank's prehistoric eye, framed by the opening in the tent, is mandarin in the moonlight. His breath rasps like an obscene caller. I can tell he is fixing to cut loose.

"Don't," I say, but it's no use.

*Eeeeeeeeehaw*!

"Frank!" I go outside, rub his nose, scratch him behind his ears, give him an apple. "I'm telling you, you've got to hold it down." I look up at Betty's lighted bedroom window. She has already warned me once tonight about this. She is afraid he'll disturb the neighbors.

It's a slippery world, my mother told me once. I remember her saying that. I am twenty-eight years old, and I should be living in a nice house, or at least a condo with a pool. Instead, I am homeless, camped out in my estranged wife's back yard, baby-sitting this neurotic mule.

I don't have a plan for tomorrow, and that is more than a little scary.

This all began when Ezra, our bass player, gave me Jonas Spencer's number. I had just split up with Betty, and I needed a place to live. A friend of Ezra's was moving out of a house Jonas owned, and Ezra said it sounded like a good deal. Jonas lived on a farm about seven miles outside the city limits. He gave me directions over the phone.

I find him sitting in a swing behind the farmhouse, an old man with sleepy-looking eyes and ears so big and hairy they don't look real. They look like fake ears people wear on Halloween. His rental house, at the end of a driveway next to his house, is a small frame building with a tin roof, front porch, and two maples for shade. A brown mule is grazing in the pasture out front.

The old man shows me around the house. With four furnished rooms, a wood stove, and a garden spot out back, it is a steal for one-twenty-five a month.

"I'd like to rent it," I say

"Fine," he says.

"Need any references?"

"Not really. You seem like a decent fellow."

I tell the old man I probably won't be there much, since my job keeps me on the road. I play guitar, harmonica, and banjo for the group the Dixie Dreamers. We travel the Southern circuit, west to Texas, north to Virginia, and south to the Florida Keys.

As it turns out, however, I spend most of the summer at home. Soon after I rent the house, a director out in L.A. hires Rex Fuller, the band's lead singer and head honcho, to score a film set in West Texas. Since the deal is strictly Rex's, and since Rex is our business manager and the only band member with a decent singing voice, that leaves the rest of us up the creek with a broken paddle. We are all plenty aggravated about this, and we call a meeting to decide what to do. After smoking a joint and drinking some wine, we decide to keep the door open to other opportunities while waiting for Rex to get back. Ezra, Roy, and Tom, the other members of the band, all share a condo in town, so their expenses aren't that high. I have some money in the bank, enough to live on until Rex gets back. I plan to write some songs and try to sell them in Nashville, learn to speak Spanish, maybe even take a trip down to Mexico. But I end up spending most of the time lying around—watching TV, reading paperback novels, playing my instruments. Weekends I hit the bars in town. I play pool, drink a few brews, and every once in awhile I get lucky and bring home a woman for the night.

While I am out on the town I keep an eye out for my wife, Betty, but I never see her: she isn't the type to hang out in a bar. She doesn't like cigarette smoke, for one thing, and she can't stand beer. I am not too happy about our separation, but what can you do about something like that? Most of the problems between Betty and me were related to my being on the road so much with the band. She wanted me to give up the band, settle down with a nine-to-five; and she wanted to have a baby. But to me there is something scary about a life like that. The time I spent away from home allowed our differences to fester, and before I knew it, I was in her lawyer's office, signing a separation agreement.

About one or two nights a week the old man comes down to the house with a six-pack and we sit on the porch and talk. Despite his satellite dish ears, the old man is a little hard of hearing. His hands are so crippled with arthritis they look like cypress knees. Sometimes he has to stand in the yard five minutes or more before he can get his urine to flow. He also has trouble with his memory. He tells me he has a fine recollection of things that happened a long time ago, like the time his father gave him a Barlow knife for his tenth birthday, but he can't remember doctors' appointments or what he got for Christmas. He says the only thing he never forgets is feeding his hogs or his mule, Frank.

Frank is an old mule, with a backbone shaped like a drawn bow, bony legs, and a scraggly tail he uses to stir up the flies. Whenever he sees the old man coming, he trots to the fence and cuts loose with one of his cacophonous, mournful brays. Frank's bray sounds like a cross between a horse's neigh and a buzz saw. The old man says when he got Frank the mule was a walking skeleton because his previous owner had kept him up in a barn all winter and only fed him every three or four days. "I feed him right regular," the old man says. "I reckon that's why he likes me so much."

When the old man comes down to the house, he always has a snack for Frank, an apple or a piece of corn bread, and if he doesn't give it to Frank right away the mule stands by the fence and brays. At first I think the old man's mule is a pain in the ass, but after awhile, I get to giving him things, too. Carrots, pancakes, honey buns. He'll eat most anything you give him. I stand by the fence while he eats and scratch him behind his long soft ears. Giving the mule food like that isn't a smart thing to do, I can see, because Frank starts raising Cain every time he sees me coming, too. I come outside to sit on the porch at night, and there he is. Snorting, tossing his head, cutting loose with a bray.

The old man rents out most of his cleared land, except for the field behind the house, where he grows corn for his hogs. The hog lot is at the end of a dirt road that runs through the field behind the house. The lot has a stream, shelter, and self-feeder. Every day the old man drives his truck down to the lot with a bag of corn. The hogs are waiting for him by the fence, squealing and grunting. The old man leans over the fence and scratches their backs while they eat.

Jonas says he worked hard all of his life with the idea of being able to take it easy and enjoy himself in his old age, but as far as he is concerned old age isn't worth much more than a pinch of owl shit. His body aches in the morning, his hearing is getting bad, his best friends are six feet under, the old woman is on his ass all the time about insignificant things, and his son and daughter never come to see him unless they want something—usually a loan that will never be paid back. If the old man gets to brooding too much about his kids, I go into the house and bring out my banjo—the old man is a fool for banjo music. I'll fingerpick a tune like "Black Mountain Breakdown," and pretty soon he is smiling and stomping his brogans.

A couple of times a week Jonas and I go fishing in the pond in the pasture across the road. The old man usually takes the mule with us and lets him graze while we fish. When we get ready to go, the old man gets ahold of Frank's bridle and leads him back across the road. I carry the string of fish.

Every so often the old woman comes down to the house and raises hell with me for drinking beer with the old man. She'll tell me how their previous tenant was a divinity student who didn't smoke or drink or have any other nasty habits, and as far as she is concerned he was a much better person to have around. And she'll accuse me of being a bad influence on the old man, whom she considers to be lazy, hateful, and generally no 'count.

One afternoon I am sitting on the porch, and I hear her shouting at Jonas in the back yard of their house. Jonas doesn't seem to be paying her much attention, but she gets so worked up she hits him in the leg with a rake. The old man gets into his truck and drives off. The old woman stands in the driveway after he leaves, shaking her fist and complaining.

That evening, he comes down to the house with a six-pack, and we sit on the porch drinking the beer, while Frank eyes us from the pasture. Jonas says the old woman is pissed at him because he talked to the Jehovah's Witnesses who paid them a visit that morning. Instead of running them off, as the old woman wanted, Jonas admits he listened to them and gave them a quarter for their magazine. But what really set the old woman off was his refusal to give her the key to his gun cabinet. She wants one of the guns in case the Jehovahs came back, only she calls them "black devils" and "crazy niggers with suitcases." The old man says the Jehovahs don't cause any harm as near as he can tell, and he doesn't see why they should be mistreated. He says that after he is gone the old woman can have all the guns she wants, and his family can sell his land to the real estate developers and live like movie stars off the money, but as long as he is alive, he is going to do things his way, and anyone who doesn't like it can go jump in the river.

I can see the old man is working himself into a state, so I go into the house for my banjo.

I really look forward to Jonas's visits. He is a good listener, especially to be old as he is. Most old people you meet would rather talk than listen. I find myself telling him personal things I've rarely told anyone, like how my father was a salesman who was gone two to three weeks out of every month, and about my mother's affair with our next-door neighbor, Norm Dixon. I tell the old man about coming home from school one day to find a note from my mother on the kitchen table. The note said she was leaving with Norm and that I could find my supper on the stove. She said there wasn't any use in looking for them because they were leaving the state. Her letter ended with, "Vance, you are fourteen now, big for your age, and I know you are able to take care of yourself."

Jonas asks me if I ever saw her again. So I tell him about the time I drove all night to see her in Baton Rouge, Louisiana, where she was managing the Mustang Motel. I knew she was there because that was the return address stamped on a postcard she'd sent me at my Aunt Lucille's. She is my father's sister who I lived with after my mother left.

When I walked into the motel I saw her sitting at the front desk. She had dyed her hair blonde, but it was my mama.

"Vance?"

"Hey, Mama."

"What a nice-looking young man you've grown up to be." I was a sophomore in college.

"How you been, Mama?"

"Call me 'Jill,' " she said, lighting a cigarette. "Can't complain. How's your father?"

"He's dead."

"How'd it happen?"

"Heart attack. Five years ago. He was trying to get home for Christmas. His heart went out on him, and he ran off the road into a ditch."

"Always figured something like that would happen to Harry. He didn't look after himself. All that fried food he ate on the road. Me, I try to eat healthy." She took a drag on the cigarette. "Got a girlfriend?"

"No one special. How's Mr. Dixon?"

"Norm is ancient history. I'm Mrs. Rossi now." She held out her hand to show me her diamond ring. "Mr. Rossi is asleep right now, on account he works the night shift; he's in security. We got a good deal here—free apartment and five hundred a month just for managing this place. Al—Mr. Rossi—helps me out when he isn't working."

"Okay." I couldn't think of anything else to say.

"I like to keep an eye on him," my mother said, giving me a wink. "It's a slippery world, Vance. Know what I mean?"

"I guess so, Mama."

"Jill."

"Sorry, I forgot."

When I finish telling the old man about my visit to see my mother in Baton Rouge, he asks if I ever hear from her.

"Not much to say now."

The old man nods solemnly.

"I don't 'spect there is," he says.


One morning in August the old woman wakes me up, pounding on the door.

"He's laying on the couch, and he won't talk," she says, scowling. The old woman reminds me of one of those little dolls made of sticks and rags, the kind they sell to tourists up in the mountains.

"Maybe he's asleep."

"Then come on and wake him up."

"I don't want to bother him," I say, and the old woman grunts and goes away.

But she is back again a while later.

"He won't eat. You'd better come talk to him. I've got work for him to do."

I follow her up to the house.

The old man is on the couch in the living room, still in his pajamas. I know what's wrong as soon as I touch his face. I close his eyes with my fingers.

"Wake him up!" The old woman's voice is shrill and scratchy, like an antique record played on a hand-cranked Victrola.

I look at the grandfather clock in the corner. I remember reading once about how clocks sometimes stop running when someone has died. Synchronicity it's called. This one appears to be working fine.

"Get up and cut the grass!" the old woman shouts into Jonas's ear.

"Jonas is dead, Mrs. Spencer."

The old woman sits in a rocking chair and looks out the window.

I sit in a chair next to the old man. With his eyes closed, he looks asleep.

"We were supposed to go fishing today," I say. There is a hard, sour lump in my throat. "He said that fish bite really good after a rain."

The old woman just sits there rocking, looking out the window.

We sit there like that for I don't know how long before I go call the old man's son.

After the old man is buried, his son and daughter hire a nurse to look after the old woman. But she keeps slipping away from the nurse and wandering around the farm, talking to herself, sticking weeds and flowers in her hair. The old man's hogs escape and roam the farm, rooting for food. I'll look out the window and see the old woman chasing them in her nightgown, waving a stick or broom in the air. I'll have to go up to the house, wake up the nurse and tell her the old woman is loose again. The two of us bring the old woman back to the house, the old woman raving about the hogs. She calls them "filthy devils."

Frank stands by the fence, braying.

I start looking for another place to live.

The old man's son, Malcolm, pays me a visit to tell me my rent is going up a hundred dollars a month. He tells me to send the check to him from now on. I tell him I am planning to move on.

"Fine by me," he says. He has the old woman's bushy eyebrows and close-set eyes.

"I've been feeding the mule," I say. "Do you think the nurse could take care of it, too?"

"I'm gonna take care of that mule," he says. " 'Bout the only thing it's good for is dog food."

Later that morning Malcom and two other men shoot the hogs, slice their throats, and haul them off in a truck. I've got to do something about Frank, I think, before Malcolm sells him to the slaughterhouse. It's the least I can do for the old man.

I pack my things into my car, rent a U-Haul, get Frank into the back of it, and drive to Betty's house.

"I need a place to keep Frank," I tell her. "Just for a few days, until I can find a home for him."

"Call the animal shelter," Betty says. She has just gotten off her nursing shift at the county hospital. "The last thing I need is a mule in my back yard."

Betty lets me use her phone to call the animal shelter. They don't take mules. I knew they wouldn't.

We sit at her kitchen table, sipping coffee. I tell her how I came into possession of Frank.

"You should have left that mule where it was," she says.

"Maybe so, but I didn't. And I've got to find a place for both of us now."

"You can't stay here, Vance. If you sleep under my roof, it will invalidate our separation agreement."

"Please help me out, Betty. For old time's sake."

"You've got a lot of nerve," she says.

But she lets me pitch a tent in her back yard.

So that's why I am here.

As I rub Frank's neck, I can smell his mule smell and feel his muscles quivering. "Take it easy, Frank," I say. "Take it easy, old boy."

I look up at Betty's bedroom window, where I know she is reading to get to sleep, and I remember how she used to pick flowers and put them on the stand by the bed for me with a little note that said, "I love you," so I would find them when I woke up. God, how sweet she was then. Where did it all go? How can love end with no warning? How can a life just disappear? Suddenly, my breath is fast and ragged. I feel like I am standing on a tightrope strung between two dead stars. One slip-up and I'm down the big rabbit hole. Just get through this moment, I tell myself. And keep the mule quiet, even if you have to stand here all night. I shut my eyes, breathe deep. My heart feels like a knotty, thorny thing, with no more purpose than this mule.

When I open my eyes, the yard is full of lightning bugs, flashing their yellow lanterns. I can feel the heat coming into my hand from the mule, who is quiet now and eating Betty's grass.

# Angles

For the first month after Bruce dumped me for a blonde with silicone implants, I spent nearly all of my time in my room, listening to my R.E.M. tapes and dreaming up plans for revenge. One of my plans was to turn up at Bruce's wedding carrying my father's pistol in my purse and shoot myself in the head just before the minister pronounced them man and wife. In this fantasy, I pictured the scene from above so I could relish the look on Bruce's face after he turned around to see me lying there in a pool of blood and brains. I also imagined putting dynamite under Bruce's waterbed and blowing him and his blonde bimbo to Kingdom Come while they were having sex. In my fantasy I had a video camera hidden in Bruce's wall, and I was able to watch everything on closed-circuit TV. Just as their moans reached peak intensity, I said, "Surprise!" and blew them up.

In my favorite fantasy I had caught some incurable disease, like leukemia or AIDS. There I am, lying in a hospital bed, my face pale and gaunt, my eyes wide and tragic and full of mysterious lights. Bruce comes in, crying. Kneeling beside my bed, he tells me he loves me and begs my forgiveness for dumping me for a blonde with fake breasts. I stroke his hair, forgive him, and die. Then I look down from the spirit world and see Bruce sobbing on my body.

The blonde's name is Tammy, and she is going to modeling school in Atlanta. Bruce met her at the swimming pool where he is a lifeguard for the summer. He had been seeing her for two weeks on the sly before I found out about it. The way I found out was, I smelled her stinky perfume on him. The first time I asked him about it, he lied and said someone had sprayed it on him at the store. The next time I asked him about the smell he claimed it was in my imagination. This led to a huge fight, after which he finally broke down and admitted everything. Although I couldn't stop crying, I did manage to question him about Tammy. He told me all about her, including his worry that she might get cancer because of her silicone implants. She had them put in for her upcoming audition as a model for Star Search. Bruce agreed with my comment that implants are a cheap way to get attention, but he added that he didn't think they were such a bad idea from a business standpoint.

Bruce said he loved me but felt like he had committed himself to me when he was too young. "I need some time to feel like a free man again, Leanne," he said. He offered to keep seeing both of us, but I told him no way, either she goes or I do, and that's when we officially broke up.

Afterwards, I couldn't eat, I couldn't sleep. In three weeks I lost the ten pounds I had been trying to lose for a year. I kept on starving myself, eating only a cup of yogurt, an apple, and a handful of raisins a day. I lost five more pounds, and my mother got so worried she asked the minister to see me.

The minister told me I was a beautiful girl who had everything to live for. He talked about the importance of being able to break our earthly attachments and put our faith in God. Which is all very easy for him to say, but I don't think he was taking my feelings into account. Bruce was my first love, my boyfriend for two and a half years, ever since our sophomore year in high school. I pictured our future together as one of categories: the Marriage, Honeymoon, Bruce's First Real Job, the Baby. I had everything planned out with such certainty that I even pictured our Retirement Years. We would spend our winters in a villa in Key West, summers in our chalet in the mountains. I had even gone so far as to decorate our villa, planning where I would put certain rugs and lamps. I imagined Bruce and I would still make love, but only about once a month.

While I listened to the minister I was imagining a scene during the Inquisition in which Bruce and Tammy were about to be beheaded for their evil ways. In this fantasy I was the executioner's daughter, and Bruce kept sneaking me messages, begging me to use my influence to spare his life.

I don't know how long I would have spent in my room, losing weight and listening to R.E.M. if I hadn't seen this ad under the help wanted section of the classifieds:

*Model needed for consortium of three clothing stores. If you are beautiful, slim, and possess unlimited ambition, see Ms. Ramsey at Dill's Clothiers, Southsquare Mall.*

I spent more than an hour putting on my makeup and combing my hair before I went down to the mall to apply for the job.

It wasn't exactly what I expected. Vicki, the woman who interviewed me, explained that the job required someone to be "a living mannequin," modeling clothes on a pedestal in the center of the mall. Part of the interview consisted of me trying on outfits and holding various poses for three to five minutes.

"It's not easy to be a mannequin," Vicki said. "It takes discipline to stand up there for two hours at a time without moving or breaking your concentration. Not only that, you have to be able to appeal to people's dream images of themselves. Being a mannequin is an art form, and the best mannequins are artists just like painters or musicians."

I went home and dreamed up a new revenge on Bruce: he became a paraplegic as the result of a car accident, and Tammy had to push him by my modeling pedestal every day on the way to physical therapy.

A couple of days after the interview Vicki called to tell me I had the job.

"I like your attitude, and you've got a great build for modeling," she said. "We can work on your technique."

The first week on my new job I suffered from cramped muscles at night, but I am getting used to it now; all I feel is a little stiffness when I get off work. I have evolved a technique that works for me. What I do is, I fix my eyes on a certain spot and concentrate on my breathing. This is a little trick I learned from Vicki. I breathe deep and slow and picture myself as a rare, exotic flower growing high above all of the noise and motion below.

I work ten to six, five days a week. I usually spend two hours wearing an outfit before I change into a new one. Vicki usually picks the outfits, but she listens to my suggestions. Last week, for example, she let me exchange a lavender scarf for a green one. The clothes are expensive and fashionable, and it's a joy to wear them, to feel them next to my skin. But the real thrill is in the comments people make when they pass. I am definitely noticed up here. Yesterday, I heard a lady say, "What a gorgeous outfit. I'd give my soul to be able to wear that."

There are also occasional ugly comments from rude people, but I ignore them. Vicki warned me I would get a certain amount of that. It's just part of the profession.

I have several poses. In my favorite pose, I am poised as if I am trying to decide what to do, which way to go. My eyes look dreamy, and my lips are pouting a little. I like this one because it's sexy and it catches people's attention. I have been working on new poses, studying real mannequins as well as models in magazines, trying to get ideas. The best poses are natural yet possess a certain dynamic quality that attracts the eye. I practice at night in front of my mirror. I am also going to aerobics class four days a week to improve my muscle tone and energy level, and I'm sticking to my diet—vegetables, yogurt, fruit, and an occasional piece of fish, cooked without butter or oil. My body is all bones and angles, but that's what it takes to look good in clothes. I have only scratched the surface of what I will need to know and do to realize my talent. I am saving my money and planning to go to modeling school, though not the same school Tammy attended. (Vicki has already told me that school is strictly second-rate, which doesn't surprise me.) I am also going to get a video made of myself modeling clothes, and I am planning to audition for *Star Search*.

Today, I saw Bruce and Tammy passing by my pedestal. She was wearing a short, black skirt and a pink, low-cut sweater that showed off her tacky fake boobs.

"Why, look," she said, "isn't that Leanne?"

Bruce nods and says, "Hey, Leanne," as they pass, but I ignore them and concentrate on my breathing.

"She looks like a real mannequin," I hear Tammy say, and my heart swells with pride.

Here is my gift, I think. This is my art.

Goodbye, Bruce, baby. Goodbye.

# Adrift

The old man's smoke-colored eye, sunken in its socket, glared at the boy standing in the hall. "What you waiting for," the old man asked, "Christmas?"

"Tell me a story, Pa-pa," Darrell said.

"Don't know no stories. Now give me that."

But the boy stayed in the hall, looking at the old man. He was sitting on the side of his bed, wearing his stained long underwear. The sunlit shade behind him was the rich, dark yellow of cured tobacco leaves. The walls were peeling, like sunburned skin. The radio on the stand beside the bed was playing a song the boy recognized, a woman singing about being crazy for loving someone. He had heard that same song playing on the jukebox in the Black Cat Tavern last week when he had gone there looking for his mother.

"You give me that right now, you hear!"

Darrell went into the room and put the pie pan of collards and corn bread into the old man's mottled hands. A network of blue veins popped out from beneath the skin like the path left by a mole. "Why can't you tell me a story?"

"Don't know no stories." More than a year had passed since the old man had told his grandson a story. Now he spent most of his time in his room, sitting in his rocker and listening to his radio. "Where's my water?"

"I forgot." Darrell went out of the room and down the hall to the kitchen. He picked up a jar from the table and, pushing open the screen door, he went down the concrete steps to the water pump near the back door. He set the jar on the ground, took the handle in both hands, and pumped it up and down, filling the jar until it overflowed. He put his mouth under the pump to catch the last of the water.

He stood up, looking at the tobacco growing in the fields around the house. Earl Morris, who owned their house and the land around it, had promised Darrell a job when the tobacco was harvested. Mr. Morris needed someone to tend the fire in one of his curing barns. Darrell had already made a mental list of things he would buy with the money: a bag of marbles, pajamas for his grandpa, a dress for Lily, and lots of food—peanut butter, ice cream, eggs, sausage, and beans.

When the boy returned to Pa-pa's room, the old man was sitting in his rocker, the empty pie pan on the nightstand by the radio.

"Here, Pa-pa."

The old man drank from the jar, water running down his stubbly chin onto the front of his long underwear.

Darrell went outside and sat on the front porch steps. He was glad there was something for the old man to eat. One day last week his grandfather had pulled leaves from the oak in the front yard, boiled them in a pot, and eaten them for supper.

Darrell had stopped attending school back in the winter. Since then he had little to do all day but take care of the old man, his mother's father, and wait for his twin sister, Lily, to get home from school. He had stopped going to school because he didn't have any shoes. As long as the weather was warm, several children had gone to school barefoot, but after the weather turned cold, all the other children had put on shoes. Lily stuffed paper into an old pair of her mother's shoes and wore them to school. Darrell was the only one in the sixth grade without shoes. He could stand the cold, but the other children's taunts were too much to endure. At first it was easy to fool his mother about his truancy, for she was spending nights at her boyfriend's house in town. If she asked why he wasn't in school, he would pretend he was sick. When his mother finally realized he hadn't been going to school at all, she whipped him with a switch. But she didn't make him return to school. She let him stay home so he could keep an eye on the old man; she was worried he might set the house on fire.

She bought Darrell a new pair of brogans, using money from the government check the old man received every month. "You won't have the excuse of no shoes next fall," she told him. "You'll be a year behind, and whose fault will that be?"

Darrell's half-brother, Marvin, who was seventeen, had always managed to get whatever he needed, and Darrell envied him for this ability. Last year, just before it turned cold, Marvin had come in carrying a pair of moldy boots he had found in a barn. There had been some baby mice in one of the boots and Marvin crushed them in the front yard with a rock. Their tiny bodies resembled crushed grapes.

Darrell didn't see Marvin much now, not since he had moved in with the Quidleys. Mrs. Quidley, who had two sons, worked at the cotton mill in town. Darrell's mother, Hazel Hewitt, had worked at the mill until last spring, when she had been fired. Since then she had been receiving monthly checks from the government, but she spent the money fast if she was drinking, which she usually was, and they would run out of food before the next check came.

They had been without food for two days when the old man had eaten the oak leaves. That was the night Darrell had walked four miles to town and gone into the tavern, looking for his mother. There were several men in the dimly lit room, but no women. "Who you looking for?" the man behind the bar asked. Darrell told him Hazel Hewitt. "I see her, I'll tell her you're looking for her," the man said.

On his way home he stole some collard greens from someone's garden. He cooked the collards for supper in the big black pot on the stove, seasoning them with lard since he didn't have any fatback.

His mother had come in late that night, and she and the old man had gotten into a fierce argument. The old man was angry because he had given her the money remaining from his monthly check, out of which the rent and electric bill were paid, to buy groceries. But after staying gone three days and two nights, all she brought home was a bag containing two bottles of wine, a bag of peanuts, and a six-pack of beer. That was one of the worst fights they had ever had, with the old man calling her a drunken whore and Hazel threatening to throw him out of the house. Darrell and Lily listened to the fight from their bed. The angry voices cracked over their heads like mirrors, showering them with splinters of unlucky glass.


Down the road he saw the yellow school bus. Soon the bus stopped in front of his house and Lily got off, walking up the dusty driveway to the porch. She wore her blue dress, which she washed every other night by hand in the washtub they used to bathe in. While the blue one was drying, she wore her other dress, yellow dotted swiss. On her feet were the shoes she had gotten for Christmas.

Putting her books and purse on the porch, she sat down beside him on the steps. She was blonde, like him, and freckled, with wide-set blue eyes. "Hey, Darrell."

"Hey."

"You eat?"

"Had some collards."

"Did you feed Pa-pa?"

"I give him some collards and corn bread."

Lily opened the purse and took out something wrapped in napkins. "I brung you this."

It was one half of a bologna sandwich, saved from the lunch she got free every day at school. He ate it slowly, savoring the meat, the spicy mustard. It was the first meat he had had in more than a week. Three weeks earlier, after his mother got her check, they had gone to the grocery store in town, Mama, Darrell, and Lily, and bought six bags of groceries. A woman who worked at the mill had driven them to the store and back. The last of that food, pintos and rice, had run out on Wednesday, two days before the old man had eaten the leaves. The only other food his mother had brought home since then was a bag of cornmeal and a can of lard.

That had been on Saturday, three days ago. That was the last time Darrell had seen her. She was off somewhere with her new boyfriend, Turner.

"Want some collards?" he asked. He had stolen them the night before from the garden of a man who lived down the road. He had tried to get some beans, too, but a light had come on in the house, and someone had fired a gun out the back door. He was lucky to get away with the collard greens.

"Maybe later," Lily said, and she got up and went into the house.

Darrell could hear the music from Pa-pa's radio, a man singing about having trouble sleeping at night. Darrell listened to the words awhile, but the song didn't make much sense. He guessed the man had a lot on his mind. Maybe he was hungry.

Later, when he went into the kitchen, Lily was eating a plate of collards at the table.

I shouldn't have eat that sandwich, he thought. She should have eat it herself.

The late-afternoon sun was a red-gold silhouette behind thick, drifting clouds. The tobacco in the fields was still, since no wind blew, and the only sound in the yard was a mockingbird singing high in the oak.

Darrell knelt beside the circle they had drawn in the dirt. Taking aim with his steely, he shot it at Lily's cat's eye in the center of the circle.

"Pow," he said, as the steely knocked the cat's eye out of the circle.

Retrieving his steely and her marble, he shot his steely at her other cat's eye. He missed.

It was Lily's turn. Kneeling, she brushed her hair out of her eyes, and, holding the marble between her thumb and forefinger, she shot it at one of Darrell's blue marbles, knocking it out of the circle. Her second shot took out another one of his blue marbles. She liked the blue ones, but Darrell didn't care much for them. He liked cat's eyes and steelies. Cat's eyes were the color of milk, with bands of color in them, red or yellow; steelies were silver. He had two cat's eyes and one steely; he had won them when he still attended school. His only chance to get more was to win them from Lily. With her third shot, Lily knocked out a big brown marble he didn't care much about.

It was his turn. He took aim and nicked her other cat's eye. Retrieving his shooter, he moved around the circle, trying to find the best position to shoot at her cat's eye.

"Yonder comes someone," Lily said.

They looked down the road, squinting at two figures walking.

"Marvin," Lily said. "And somebody else."

Quickly, they picked up the marbles and put them into Darrell's red bandanna, which he crammed into his pocket. They went up to the porch and sat in the two cane chairs by the door.

"Trent Quidley," Lily said.

Trent Quidley was sixteen, the older of the two Quidley boys. He had already been in jail twice, once for beating up a teacher.

Darrell and Lily were silent as Marvin and Trent entered the yard. They both wore faded jeans and T-shirts. Despite the heat Marvin had on his black boots.

"What was you all doing down in the dirt?" he asked, as he came up the steps.

"Nothing," Darrell said.

"Want me to punch your face?"

"We wasn't doing nothing."

"Lie to me, I'll kick your ass," Marvin said, showing off in front of Trent.

"Ought to kick his ass anyway," Trent said. His nose looked like it had been broken and healed crooked.

Marvin grabbed Darrell by his arm, jerking him to his feet. "What you got in your pocket?"

"You leave him be!" Lily came toward them, but Trent jumped up onto the porch and blocked her path.

"Where you going, blondie?"

Marvin twisted Darrell's arm behind his back until he cried out. "Want me to break it?"

Lily tried to run past Trent, but he caught her and lifted her in the air.

103

"Let me go!" She kicked her thin legs against him.

"She-cat," Trent said.

"Give me what you got in your pocket," Marvin said.

With his free hand Darrell took out the handkerchief containing the marbles and dropped it on the porch.

When Marvin let him go, Darrell tackled Trent, knocking him backwards off the porch. Trent landed on his back, with Lily on top of him, Darrell still holding on to his knees.

Trent pushed Lily off and pinned Darrell beneath him. Darrell kicked and bucked, trying to throw Trent off, but the older boy was too heavy and strong.

He could see Trent's red face above him. Lily had her arms around his neck.

"Get that she-cat, Marvin!"

Marvin grabbed Lily and held her while Trent choked him. As Darrell looked up at Trent, the sky behind him faded into pinpoints of light floating on a sea of darkness. His strength slipping away, he felt his soul float out of him, up into the tree with the mockingbird.

"Darrell, Darrell!"

When he opened his eyes his head was in Lily's lap. Someone was shouting.

It was Trent, running in the yard, Pa-pa behind him, slicing the air with his sword, the unbuttoned flap on the seat of his long underwear bouncing up and down, revealing his gaunt buttocks.

"Marvin! Get this crazy son of a bitch off me, you hear? Marvin!"

But Marvin wasn't in sight.

The old man chased Trent into the road, then stood in the yard, brandishing the Confederate sword he kept under his bed. He was threatening to cut out Trent's liver and feed it to the crows.

"Marvin!" Trent cried. "Marvin!"

Marvin ran around the side of the house, carrying the old man's radio under his arm. He danced in the road, while the old man rained curses on them. Marvin held up the radio, shaking it like a tambourine.

"You give Pa-pa back his radio!" Darrell cried hoarsely. His neck and throat hurt.

Marvin tossed the radio to Trent, who slammed it down on the road. He picked it up, slammed it down again, and kicked it into the ditch. Then he and Marvin ran backwards toward town, jeering at the old man, who stood in the road, waving the sword and cursing them.

A ray of sunlight, shining down through a hole in the clouds, caught the sword so that for a moment it looked like the old man was holding a wand of flaming light.

"Defend the poor and fatherless," Lily read, "do justice to the afflicted and needy. Deliver the poor and needy: rid them out of the hand of the wicked. They know not, neither will they understand; they walk on in darkness: all the foundations of the earth are out of course. I have said Ye are gods; and all of you are children of the most High."

Darrell lay in bed, watching a moth circling the candle on the stand. As usual, he wasn't paying much attention to his sister's passages from the Bible. She had begun the nightly readings after he quit going to school. The moth ignited its wings on the flame and made a fiery descent to the floor, like a bad angel falling out of Heaven.

Lily finished reading and blew out the candle.

"Do you remember what book that was from?" she asked.

"No."

"Psalms. You should pay more attention to the word of God."

"I ain't never seen him."

"Hush." She kicked him under the sheet. "Don't talk like that. You're s'posed to fear Him."

"Who says?"

"The Bible says, and it's His holy word."

They lay there listening to the cicadas and crickets outside, Darrell thinking of the things he was afraid of: Trent and Marvin; a one-eyed monster coming out of the woods at night and eating him alive; his mama, Lily, or Pa-pa dying; falling into a well with no way to get out and no one to hear his cries for help. With all those things to fear, it didn't seem fair that he had to fear God, too. He could see the moonlit outline of the metal frame on the dresser. The frame contained a drawing of their father whom they had never seen. He was a traveling man who sold caskets, according to their mother. "He was just passing through," she had said. "It won't no serious thing." Hazel had sketched their father one night, using a pen and a sheet of notebook paper, after Darrell and Lily asked her to describe him.

Darrell looked out the window at the tobacco, luminescent now under the copper-colored moon. When the wind blows they look like waves, he thought. A dog was howling in the distance.

"Seems funny, not hearing Pa-pa's radio," he said.

"I'm gonna buy him another one for Christmas," Lily said.

"How you gonna get the money?"

"I'm praying for it."

"Won't do no good."

"The Bible says you can move a mountain with a seed of faith."

"Maybe so, but I'm gonna buy him one before Christmas."

"With what?"

"Money I make working in 'bacca for Mr. Morris."

"You better be in school this fall, you hear me, Darrell? You done lost a year already."

Darrell didn't answer. He was remembering how it was before their mother's drinking problem got bad and she lost her job at the mill. This was back during the time when his grandfather told him the stories. Their mother would cook suppers of fried chicken or country-style steak, collards, yams, hot biscuits, and apple pie. At night they would eat ice cream or watermelon on the front porch. Marvin, Lily, and Darrell slept in the same room, Marvin, in his bed, Lily and Darrell in theirs. At night, their mother would come in and kiss them good night.

Darrell fell asleep and dreamed of silver coins falling from the tree in the front yard. Every time a gust of wind blew, the tree would let loose a shower of more silver coins.

He woke up, listening.

He heard it again, a car door slamming.

Then he heard voices outside: his mama and Turner, talking on the front porch. Turner was a mechanic at a garage in town.

Darrell got up, went down the hall, and stared through the screen at them sitting on the porch. There was a paper bag beside his mama on the porch. He hoped she had brought some groceries home.

She was complaining about Pa-pa. "His mind is about gone. Half the time he can't even remember his own name. It's a wonder he can still wipe himself."

"Ought to put him in the county home," Turner said.

"Scared he'd burn it down," Hazel said, and they laughed.

"Mus-skeeters is eating me up," Turner said.

When they got up to come into the house, Darrell slipped into Pa-pa's room, which smelled sour. He expected his grandfather to be asleep, but the old man was sitting in his chair. "Whoring! In front of her own children."

Darrell sat on the floor beside his grandpa's chair, listening to the footsteps going down the hall to the kitchen. The broken radio was on the nightstand, the tubes glowing red in the darkness.

"She's riding that bottle down to hell!"

"Tell me a story, Pa-pa."

"What?"

"A story. Like you used to tell me."

"Can't remember any stories."

"Tell me about the time you lost your eye."

"My eye?"

"You said you was fighting in the war."

"I got hurt at the mill," the old man said.

Darrell was disappointed that the old man wouldn't tell him about losing his eye in hand-to-hand combat with a German soldier armed with a bayonet. Although Darrell knew that story to be untrue, he liked to hear it anyway. He missed the time in his life when the old man used to tell him stories. Stories about fighting in wars, working in the mill, where he had been a loom fixer, and growing up on the coast, where his father had been a fisherman.

Darrell's favorite story was about the time his great-grandfather, a fisherman named John Hewitt, got lost at sea. John Hewitt had been fishing off the coast of South Carolina when his boat capsized in a storm. He and his two-man crew escaped in a lifeboat, and every day they waited for help to arrive. But no help came. They survived by drinking rainwater caught in a bucket and eating the small fish that occasionally jumped over their bow. As the days stretched into weeks, the men lost so much weight that they looked like skeletons with skin stretched over the bones. The two crewmen began to go mad. They fought with each other and with John Hewitt, and they imagined they saw ships on the horizon. They finally jumped into the sea and drowned. Then, John Hewitt began hearing and seeing the ghosts of the drowned men. They kept appearing in the boat and urging him to join them in the water, tempting him with promises of food hidden in chests on the ocean floor. But John refused to give in to them. To keep his sanity he sang and prayed, and in the middle of his second month adrift at sea, he was rescued by a Navy ship. "He never give up," the old man had said, "on account of he was a Hewitt, and Hewitts is stubborn that way."

"Pa-pa," Darrell said. "Do you remember the story about the time your daddy got lost at sea?"

"Did he get lost at sea?" the old man asked.

Darrell went back to his room. Opening the closet door, he saw light streaming through the hole in the wall, put there years earlier when a shotgun Marvin's father had been cleaning went off by accident. Darrell put his eye to the hole and he could see his mama sitting at the table. She sat hunched over her glass, smoking a cigarette, her hair in her eyes. She only smoked when she was drinking. Sober, her voice was usually soft and even a little musical, but after she started drinking, her voice became more harsh and she used ugly words. She also complained about people who had hurt her, especially Hugh Tanner, Marvin's father. Although she had only known Darrell and Lily's father a few months, she had lived with Hugh for seven years. The last Darrell had heard, Hugh was in Louisiana, working on the offshore oil rigs.

Now she was complaining about Pete Crawford, the supervisor who had fired her from the cotton mill where she had worked for as long as Darrell could remember.

"That goddamned Pete Crawford ruined my life. Told him I got kids to take care of—you think that bothered him? Hell, no. He said, 'Hazel, we're running a business here. We can't allow people to just show up when they feel like it.' Son of a bitch didn't believe I'd been sick."

"Pete Crawford so much as look at me funny, I'll punch his face," Turner said. Darrell could see his big-knuckled hands on the table.

Hazel laughed. She opened the bag and took out a bottle of wine.

Turner crumpled up the bag and threw it on the floor.

No groceries, Darrell thought angrily, as he watched her pour wine into the glass. Why didn't she bring some food home?

He was hungry, and the collards were gone now. But his mama was here at least. In the morning when she woke up, he could tell her he was hungry, and if she had any money left maybe they would go into town and buy some groceries. If she didn't have any money, her check from the government would arrive soon. I can hold out until then, he thought.

He went back to his bed and imagined what he would eat when they came back from the store. Fried eggs and thick strips of bacon, and four or five hotcakes dripping with butter, and he would wash it down with milk, lots of milk. For dessert he would eat a candy bar and drink another glass of milk.

He could hear Lily breathing, feel her body warm against his. He pictured his great-grandfather adrift in the small boat, surrounded on all sides by endless green water and above him, the empty blue sky. Darrell imagined John Hewitt catching fish in his hands as they jumped over the bow, drinking rain water out of a bucket and arguing with the two dead men who had come back to try to kill him. Pa-pa couldn't remember so good any more, but that was all right: Darrell would remember for him. He could see that his great-grandfather's story was part of him now, like his eyes or his hands, like his beating heart.

# Silhouette

I am in my cubicle, trying to finish a report Preston wants by five o'clock, when my concentration is broken by an angry voice in the hall: "Just listen to me, dammit! Listen to me when I talk." I look out and see Cicero Jones holding his wife, Althea, by the arm. She struggles to get away, but his grip is too firm. He has the massive chest and thick neck of a weightlifter.

"Cicero, you're embarrassing me," Althea says. "Let's talk about this at home."

"Home? We got no home. It's a goddamned tomb, baby. You hear me? A tomb!"

My colleagues are peering out from their offices. I see Ed Colby, a specialist in city planning, poke his face out then disappear into his office. Gail Ashley shakes her head, frowns, looks at me helplessly.

Cicero's shaved head glistens under the fluorescent lights. The armpits of his denim shirt are black with sweat. What the hell is wrong with him? He must be drunk. I want to do something to help, but what? I return to my office, thinking I am only embarrassing Althea further by witnessing the conflict with her husband.

All this week she has been withdrawn and melancholy. Just yesterday I told her if she ever needed to talk, I would be glad to listen. "Thanks, Nate," she said, forcing a smile. "I'll keep that in mind." A graphic artist, Althea helps the art director produce the brochures, newsletters, and other publications we do here at the Southern Institute for Public Policy.

I sit back at my desk, feeling guilty for not trying to help her resolve the disagreement with her husband. Although I jog regularly and play racquetball at the health club, I realize if things got physical I would be no match for Cicero, who must outweigh me by seventy-five pounds. I try to concentrate on my report, remembering the tension in Preston's voice when he asked me to have it ready by five today. Preston, our director, was supposed to have written the report to the Institute's board of directors himself, but once again I have ended up doing his work. He gave me his notes late yesterday afternoon—an incoherent jumble of ideas. I was here until midnight and back again at 7:15 this morning, working on the report. Preston claimed he was unable to get to it due to an important meeting with a potential donor. He's known about the report for weeks, however, and, as usual, he dropped it in my lap at the last minute.

More loud angry voices. Then a scream and the sounds of scuffling. Rushing out to the hall I see Stella Hubert tackle Cicero, who is holding Althea by the hair. Her head is bent back, exposing her sinewy throat.

Cicero grabs Stella by the hair too, pulling her to her feet. Her face is crimson. He releases her hair, places his palm against her chest and shoves her down the hall toward me.

"Stella, let me handle this!"

Sneering, as if I am the enemy, too, Stella says, "Oh, yeah? Look!"

Turning, I see Cicero dragging Althea by her arm along the polished floor toward the elevator, where a group of onlookers stands. Althea's body is limp, her eyes closed, her face streaked with tears. Preston—in the doorway to the office lounge, watching them pass by—looks like a man stricken with intestinal pain. He takes the white handkerchief from the breast pocket of his navy blazer and daubs his forehead.

I rush down the hall after them.

As Cicero drags Althea past Ted Harmon's office, Ted springs out and wraps his long slim body around Althea's. "Stop hurting her!"

"I'm gone hurt you, fool!" Cicero raises his right arm like a club above Ted's head.

When I put my hand on Cicero's shoulder, the muscles beneath his skin feel like steel cables. "Cicero, let's talk about what's upsetting you. You don't really want to hurt Althea."

I expect to be decked by one of his huge fists, but instead Cicero only nods, his red-veined eyes fill with tears. "You're right," he says. He reeks of stale beer and sweat.

"Just let her go. We can talk about all this. We can go into the conference room and talk it out."

"What about me? Huh? Everybody's worried about her. What about me?"

While I am trying to think of a response, Ted makes a sudden effort to pull Althea free. Cicero leans over and punches Ted behind his right ear. Ted falls to the floor, groans once, lies still.

Althea screams.

The people at the elevator just stand there, staring at us. A man in a security officer's uniform is among them. Jesus, I think, why doesn't someone try to help?

"Cicero," I say. "This is Althea, your wife, not your enemy. She is someone you love, and you must let her go. Do you hear me? Just let her go."

"I just can't stand this shit no more, man," he says, shaking his head. Know what I'm saying?"

"I want you to tell me about it, Cicero. Tell me what you can't stand."

"I—I don't even know where to start."

"Just tell me how you feel. That's as good a place as any." I want to keep him talking until the police get here. Surely someone has called them.

Stella again—on Cicero's broad back like a monkey, clawing at his face.

Cicero reaches up behind him and seizes her hair. He swings her over his shoulder, slamming her against the floor.

Stella wheezes, struggling to get her breath.

"You bastard!" Althea cries.

"Bitch jumped me, what you talking about?" Cicero has a red scratch on his cheek.

"Cicero!" I say firmly, placing my hand again on his shoulder. "Let's talk about this!"

"Talk, talk—everybody wants to talk about her. What about me? Am I garbage?"

"You're her husband."

Cicero looks at me as if he's seeing me for the first time. "Where you been, man? Where the hell you been?"

Out of the corner of my eye I see the elevator door open. God, let it be the police.

But it's only Al Potts, who works at the accounting firm on the first floor. The bystanders fall all over themselves getting on the elevator.

Al saunters up as if everything in the world is right and good, as if there are no terrorists plotting to poison the nation's water supplies and blow up our cities, as if the whole planet isn't polarized by deep divisions—between Palestinian and Jew, rich and poor, black and white, women and men—and as if Cicero isn't holding his sweet sobbing wife Althea now by the hair. Al greets Cicero with a breezy, "What's up, bro?"

"Man, this shit done got the best of me. Know what I'm saying?"

"Most definitely. Shit will do that to a man." Al comes up to our floor sometimes to see Ed Colby, with whom he plays racquetball.

"He's a little upset with Althea," I say, feeling a deep gratitude for Al's presence, the implicit power conveyed to the dilemma by his brown skin. "I've been trying to get him to talk it out."

"Why don't you let me talk to him? Sometimes it takes a brother to understand a brother." Al says this with such an easy, casual grace that I cannot feel offended, only relief at being able to turn this crisis over to him.

Al and Cicero exchange a soul brother handshake, a series of arcane moves that concludes with them slapping each other's palms.

"Let's go outside, get out of this place," Al says.

"What for?"

"Too many folk with big ears."

"Right." Cicero nods and lets go of Althea's hair. "Althea, listen—"

"Go away," she says. "Just please go away."

"I'll talk to you later," he says. Then he and Al walk down the hall toward the elevator.

Ed Colby comes out of his office, and we both help Stella to her feet. We ask her if she is all right.

"I'm okay," she says. "Just had the breath knocked out of me. What about Ted?"

Ted is still on his back, his eyes closed, Althea kneeling beside him. I squat beside her, touch his face. We call his name.

His eyelids flutter. "Althea."

"How you feeling, baby?" she asks, squeezing his hand.

"Okay, I guess." Ted eats lunch occasionally with Althea. She advises him on his love life. He sits up, rubbing the area behind his ear. "Anybody get the license number?"

"Ted, honey, I'm so sorry," Althea says. She strokes his arm, his shoulder. Her hands are fine and lovely, with slender, conic fingers. She has a jade cross in the fleshy part of her earlobe. I inhale her scent: a mixture of sweat and that woodsy perfume she wears. I can't remember when I have last been this close to a woman. I have an almost overpowering urge to enfold her in my arms, kiss her tears away.

Ted insists on standing. Ed, Stella, and I help him up. "My mama always said I had a hard head," he says.

Althea sits on the floor, her back against the wall. "Lord Jesus," she says, wiping tears from her eyes.

More staff members are leaving their cubicles. The women kneel like magi around Althea. Down the hall Cicero and Al get on the elevator, the door sliding shut behind them.

Feeling lightheaded, I return to my office, put my face down on my desk. My heart thuds wildly in my chest—an empty, hollow thing.

All the next day Cicero's attack on Althea, Ted, and Stella is the main topic of conversation around the office. Jay Caps, who refers to Ted as "our gay vegetarian," says he is thinking about getting a concealed weapon permit for his pistol, due to all the crazies running around loose. Several staff members are afraid Cicero will return after he gets out of jail. The deputies arrested him without incident by the wooden tables out back, where he and Al were talking

Preston, who had been useless during the crisis, makes an attempt to restore order and a semblance of leadership. After lunch, he calls a staff meeting in the conference room to announce that has hired a counselor to help us cope with the "unfortunate disruption of our work environment." Conspicuously absent are Ted, Stella, and Althea, all of whom spent yesterday afternoon in the emergency room: Ted with a mild concussion; Stella with bruises and a cracked rib; Althea with sprained muscles and a pinched nerve in her neck. Although Althea takes the rest of the week off, Stella and Ted are back at work two days later. Stella tells me that Althea's problems with her husband began two months ago, after he was laid off from his job at a warehouse. Unable to find another job, he had been sitting around the house, drinking beer and feeling sorry for himself. The trouble in the office had started when Cicero had come to get Althea for lunch. Althea was working on a deadline and didn't want to leave. The argument had spun out of control from there.

I am concerned about how long it took the deputies to respond: more than twenty-five minutes after the first call went in, someone says. According to Preston the deputies claimed the caller hadn't provided clear directions.

Clear directions? The Institute for Public Policy is on the third floor of a four-story modern steel and glass building right off the interstate. The deputies who took our statements seemed professional enough, but the long response time is unnerving. Had Cicero been homicidal and armed, he could have killed everyone on the floor.

I am reminded of my Uncle Darren, who keeps a sawed-off shotgun under his bed. "World is a jungle nowadays," he says. "Two-legged predators everywhere. Pays to be prepared."

Once I heard my mother argue with him about this.

"What about the police?" She'd said. "It's their job to protect people. That's what they get paid to do."

"Cops only get there after you're dead," my uncle said. "In time to draw the outline of your body on the floor."

I don't want to live like that. In constant fear. And yet how can I avoid it? Cicero's attack on Althea has changed the way I feel about my work place. What's to stop him—or anybody for that matter—from bursting in with a high-capacity weapon and venting his rage and sense of powerlessness by pumping bullets into our bodies?

I wonder if any of us will ever feel safe here again.

The man in the security uniform was an animal control officer, responding to a complaint about a stray dog that had been foraging in the trash cans by the wooden tables outside. He had gotten off on the wrong floor.

Our session with the counselor takes place in the conference room at the end of the hall opposite the elevator. Preston sits at his customary place at the head of the mahogany table, a freshly pressed white handkerchief in the breast pocket of his gray flannel suit coat. He wears a banana-colored tie, blue shirt, gold cuff links. The rest of us sit around the table. The counselor, a woman with frosted hair, has the precise elocution of a television news anchor. Standing by a portable blackboard, she begins by talking about post-traumatic stress syndrome, a condition she says we are all suffering from. She tells us that we may be feeling depressed and irritable and have trouble sleeping. We may crave sweets, other comfort foods, or alcohol, but indulging in these things will only make the problem worse.

The counselor believes it would be a good idea for each of us to release our emotions about the incident. To prompt us, she suggests we tell what we were doing when Cicero came in, how we reacted to the event, and how we are feeling now.

Stella says she was afraid Cicero was going to kill Althea, which was why she had attacked him. Since then she has been having trouble sleeping at night, and she has gone back on an antidepressant.

Other employees make brief, predictable comments: they were afraid, concerned about Althea's welfare, frustrated because they weren't sure how to respond. Lorraine Manning, one of two staff members who had called 911, said she was especially disturbed that the attack had taken place in the office, a place she had always associated with stability and order.

Ted Harmon is even more personal.

"When I was little my father used to beat my mother," he says, looking down at his hands. "When I saw Cicero assaulting Althea, all those beatings came back. I didn't care what happened to me. I just didn't want Althea to be hurt. I wanted to take the punishment for her."

The uncomfortable silence that follows is broken by the nasal voice of Jay Capps, who had been out of the office during the attack. "What I'm feeling is guilt. I feel like I should have been here to protect you all from this scumbag."

The counselor nods vigorously. "So you are feeling guilt because you weren't here to protect the others."

"Yeah, I feel like—well—a failure."

I sigh, roll my eyes. Who is he kidding? Cicero would have put him down with one punch. I remember Jay sabotaging my last project by undermining me with Preston, the numerous times he has criticized staff members behind their backs. With his hairy ears and his devotion to Internet porn sites, who would look to him for help in a time of crisis? His primary success here is tied to his ability to bring in grant money.

While the counselor speaks to Jay in a syrupy voice, I look out the window, at a patch of green lawn below, and recall Cicero's tormented eyes, his sour smell of defeat. *What about me?*

Preston's whiny, self-righteous voice intrudes on my reverie: "My role was basically that of concerned bystander. I couldn't tell exactly what was going on. I just didn't have a clue . . ." What a perfect description of his role here at the Institute. Preston doesn't have a clue about anyone's true value or what is really going on, even though he makes twice as much money as anyone else. Except for Jay, fund raiser extraordinaire.

When the counselor calls on me, I only shake my head, having resolved to remain silent, but I suddenly find myself speaking.

"I realize this might sound heretical, but I have compassion for Cicero. And I don't think we should demonize him. He was wrong, sure, and he'll have to pay the price for his anger and loss of control. He's paying for it right now. His main problem is he doesn't know how to handle his emotions. Marriage—any close, intimate relationship with another person—is a pressure cooker. It can break down the best of us. This man has lost his job, probably lost his wife, too, and he's in jail facing serious charges. Right now he's probably wondering how his life has become so unraveled. But I don't think he's all that different from any one of us. Given the right set of circumstances, we could lose our grip too—let our frustration and rage overtake our good sense and find ourselves in the same boat."

"Speak for yourself, Nate," Jay says. "Unlike that ape, I'm not in the habit of beating up women."

"No, you act out your macho nature in other ways, Jay. Like bragging about much money you make and seeing every male you meet as a potential rival. When you get right down to it, most men—all of us, really—fall short of the civilized ideal."

"Now see here!" Jay, red-faced, quickdraws his index finger, aims it at me like a pistol. "I'll not have you impugning my character!"

"Gentlemen, please," the counselor says. "Let's focus on the central issues."

No one says anything. Preston mops his forehead with his handkerchief. Catching my eye, Ted Harmon winks.

Love is a dangerous thing, I think that night, as I lie on my cot in the kitchen by the fire escape. The AC in my building is broken, so I have moved my guest cot out here, to get the faint breeze from the window overlooking the alley. The air is tainted with the smell of garbage. I can hear two cats yowling below. The window provides me with a view of the building across the alley, a rectangle of chalky sky above. The city's lights obliterate the stars. After awhile the cats fall silent, and I can hear the distant wail of a siren. I am thirty-two years old, and I have been in love three times in my life. Each of the relationships ended badly. At certain moments toward the end, I realize I was angry and frustrated enough to do what Cicero did— seize my estranged lover by her hair. What stopped me? Why does one person snap under the pressure of feeling love slip away and another endure the loss silently, like a flower wilting in a drought? Once I was packing up to leave a woman, an artist named Ursula whom I loved but couldn't live with, and she began hurling knives at me from the kitchen drawer. A butcher knife appeared in the wall inches from my face, the handle swinging back and forth with chilling power. Ursula flew into the bedroom, locking the door behind her. I remembered the double-barreled shotgun in the closet—passed down from my grandfather but still in working order. There was a box of shells somewhere in there, too. I rushed to the bedroom, rattling the door-knob, calling her name. But she was silent. I threw my weight against the door. Ursula had been peering at me through the keyhole, and the force of the door breaking open knocked her to the floor, where she lay as if dead. I carried her to the bed and revived her with cold compresses, after which she cried and begged me not to leave. She claimed to have no memory of hurling knives at me. Ursula was a Zen Buddhist, praised for her delicate watercolors. Yet in a fit of rage she had nearly blinded me. Or worse.

A light comes on in a room across the alley, and I see a figure silhouet-ted against the shade. I wonder if it is the jogger I sometimes see running in my neighborhood, a lithe, young woman who always wears a green head-band. She smiles at me when our eyes meet. The figure behind the shade appears to be disrobing—yes, I see her taking off her bra. If it is the jogger, I would like to get to know her better. Perhaps I could invite her to lunch or suggest we run together. Surely she wouldn't mind having a partner. No strings attached, no pressure, just someone to run with.

I have been living in this apartment building for two years now, and I think of how little I know about my neighbors. On my floor there's Ms. Weitz, a retired teacher, who walks her Yorkshire terrier every morning, picking up his droppings with a plastic scooper and depositing them in a plastic bag she carries with her. She has a son in Florida. I have never known him to visit her. A man and woman moved in next door a few months ago. Sometimes I hear them quarreling through the walls. I hear them laughing, too, and making love. At the end of the hall is a couple with two boys, perhaps nine and eleven. They rarely go outside. What do they do all day? Watch TV, play computer and video games? I should try to get to know these people, I think, become part of a community. But I have no idea how to even begin doing this.

I recall a photo on Althea's desk, of her and Cicero on their honeymoon in Cancun. Her arms encircle his chest, and she is smiling as if she has found the answer to all her dreams. Now Cicero is in jail and Althea is seeing a lawyer about a restraining order and a separation agreement. I wonder if she and Cicero will ever be able to find their way back to the beginning, when their love was green and blooming and full of light.

The cats are yowling again. The woman behind the shade across the alley stretches languidly. I imagine she is the jogger, imagine she knows I am watching and that she is hoping I will make the first move.

# Prowlers

The summer I turned thirteen my mother and I were living in a white, single-story house in Chattanooga, Tennessee. The house was surrounded by wisteria bushes, and the purple blossoms drenched the air with a fragrance I could smell half a block away. My father had been gone thirteen months, and we had no idea where he was.

He was a used-car salesman who changed jobs often, and this had resulted in us moving around a lot. The worst thing about that was always being the new kid in school. I didn't make friends quickly, and if you are a new kid, the other students tend to treat you like you have an extra eye in your forehead. I wasn't happy about being a new kid again. We had spent nearly two years in Anniston, Alabama, and I had some good friends there I hated to leave behind. My father, however, was very excited because Chattanooga was the seventh city we had lived in. "Seven is a lucky number," I remember him saying, "and this will be our lucky town."

But Chattanooga turned out to be an unlucky place for us. My mother and father argued constantly, he began staying out late at night, and after my mother accused him of having a girlfriend he packed his suitcases and moved out. My mother said he was living with a redheaded floozy in the Orleans Hotel. When I went there to see him, I learned my father had checked out, leaving no forwarding address.

My mother changed after my father left. She would look off into space while I was talking to her and later not remember anything I had said. About once a month she would fly into a rage, usually over some insignificant thing, and break all of the dishes and glasses in the kitchen. While she was hurling the dishes and glasses against the wall, she would curse and complain about my father, her job, her boss, me, and life in general, and she would threaten to kill herself by jumping in front of a train. After the last of the dishes and glasses had been smashed, my mother would run into her bedroom, and, locking the door behind her, she would lie on her bed and cry. I would knock on the door and beg her to let me in. If she responded at all it would be to say, "Go away and leave me alone."

I would clean up the mess in the kitchen. When my mother came out of her room, she would have calmed down considerably. She would say something like, "My nerves haven't been good lately, Del. I've been working too hard, and I need a rest." We would eat on paper plates and drink out of cutoff milk cartons until my mother replaced the things she had broken.

Another strange thing about my mother was she was convinced there were prowlers in our yard at night. She insisted all the shades be pulled down and the curtains closed by sunset, and she often imagined she heard footsteps outside the windows. Some mornings I saw her inspecting the yard for footprints. Her prime suspects were the residents of Mr. Culpepper's rooming house next door: several toothless old men who spent their days whittling in cane-backed chairs in the front yard. My mother suspected one or more of the old men of standing outside her window at night and trying to watch her undress or use the bathroom. Although I considered my mother to be quite beautiful, I did not believe the old men were trying to look in our windows at night. When I told her this, she flew hot.

"You're still a child, Del," she said. "There are many things you don't understand."

"Those men aren't interested in much of anything except whittling."

"You don't know the way they look at me when I walk by."

The next time my mother and I walked by the rooming house I carefully searched the old men's faces for signs that would confirm them as prowlers, but the men only nodded politely at my mother, said "Hey, Del" to me, then went back to their whittling.

My mother was forty-eight years old but she looked younger, maybe forty-one or forty-two. She had lovely, chestnut-colored hair, full, firm breasts, a slim waist, and shapely legs. She worked as a secretary for a lawyer downtown, and she would often tell me about men who had asked her out. She was usually quick to add, however, that she declined the invitation because she was still married to my father, although during all the time he had been gone the only word we had received from him was a postcard wishing us well and saying he was planning to open his own business. "I'm living in a country now where a man has a chance to be who he really is," he wrote. The postcard, which had a Houston, Texas, postmark, had been addressed to my mother, but at the bottom my father had penned a brief reference to me: *Tell Del to keep his nose clean and stay out of trouble.*

My father's postcard was a scene of a cactus with a train in the background. I taped it above my bed, and whenever I looked at it I imagined my father as an unseen part of the landscape. In the train perhaps, or sitting on a horse behind it. I pictured him wearing a Stetson hat, a leather vest, and boots with silver spurs that jingled when he walked. And if someone asked about him, I'd say, "He's working as a cowboy out West. We're going to go live with him as soon as he gets settled."

One evening when my mother came home from work, she showed me a pearl-handled pistol she had borrowed from her boss. "I got this for protection," she said. "A woman was found murdered in an alley near my office building, and I'm determined nothing like that is going to happen to me. If I was dead who would take care of you?"

Without knowing it, my mother had zeroed in on my greatest fear. Ever since my father had left, I had been worried about losing her, too. Every morning when I kissed her goodbye I was afraid I would never see her again. I worried that she would be killed by a car, struck dead by a bolt of lightning, or just leave me the way my father had. What would happen to me, then? My mother had a sister I thought I could live with, but that gave me little solace. With my father gone I felt like my mother was all I had left, and I was deeply afraid of facing life without her. The fear of losing my mother preyed on my mind that summer, for I was out of school and not doing much except reading mysteries, whittling with the men down at Mr. Culpepper's rooming house, playing with my cat, Sugarfoot, or riding my bicycle around the neighborhood with my friend, Mutt Jimson. Sometimes Mutt and I would go swimming in the public pool or catch a matinee at one of the movie theaters downtown.

Early in the summer Mutt and I had made some wine out of cherries from the tree in his back yard. We let it ferment six weeks in some old jelly jars in his basement. Then we poured it in some empty root beer bottles and rode around the neighborhood on our bicycles, swilling the wine, giggling, war-whooping, and calling every girl we saw "hot lips," and "honey britches." After my tire went flat, we hid my bike in some bushes, and I rode perched on Mutt's handlebars, the bottles of our homemade wine rattling in his basket below. Then Mutt crashed his bike into a tree, knocking out two of my teeth. In our drunken state, even this was a source of humor to us. We sat there laughing at me spitting out streams of blood, and Mutt wanted us to crash into the tree again to see if I could knock out more teeth. He laughed so hard he wet his pants.

A few days later, Mutt came over to see me. My mother was in the living room, talking on the phone. We went into my mother's bedroom to discuss what we were going to do with the remaining wine in Mutt's basement. We sat on the side of her bed, the door shut so my mother couldn't hear our discussion. She was still angry with me for knocking out my teeth, and I didn't want to give her any further cause for aggravation. Sugarfoot had followed us in and was sitting beside me on the bed, purring while I scratched his back and every now and then taking kittenish swipes at a book my mother had been reading. Through the open window I could hear the bees buzzing around the wisteria. Mutt wanted us to sell our wine for fifty cents a bottle at the neighborhood youth center, and he suggested we split the money seventy-thirty since the cherries had come from his tree and the wine had been stored in his basement. I didn't like this at all, and I told him so, pointing out that not only had I done half of the work I'd also supplied the root beer bottles. "I think we should keep the wine for ourselves," I said.

We were arguing about this when Mutt slid his hand under my mother's pillow and came up with the pistol. "What's this?"

"It's for prowlers," I said. "And be careful, it's loaded."

He aimed the pistol at my heart.

"I think we should sell our wine and split the money seventy-thirty," he said. "Any arguments?"

I snatched the pistol out of his hand and from the handle I extracted the magazine containing the seven shiny bullets. My mother had showed me how to use the pistol in case someone overpowered her before she could get to it.

"Let's see it," Mutt said, and I handed it back to him. "My old man has a gun like this, only bigger. He killed a Jap with it. Shot him through the eye."

Mutt cocked the pistol by pulling back the slide. Then he pointed it at my chest and pulled the trigger. The pistol went *click*. Grinning, he cocked it again, aimed it at my face and clicked it again.

I took it away from him, inserted the magazine in the handle and slid the gun back under my mother's pillow. "Let's talk business," I said. "I'm willing to sell part of the wine, but I think fifty-fifty is fair."

"You're dreaming, Del."

We argued awhile longer without making any headway. I got up to use the bathroom, and when I returned Mutt had the pistol in his hand again.

"Give me that," I said, and I took it away from him.

"I just want to hold it," he said, so I extracted the magazine, slipped it into my pocket and handed him the pistol.

"I'd like to borrow this sometime."

"It's not ours to loan. Belongs to my mother's boss."

"No one will ever know about it. I can just keep it awhile then bring it back."

"That gun stays here," I said.

"Don't argue with me," Mutt said, pointing the muzzle at my chest.

"I'm not arguing, just stating a fact."

Mutt aimed the pistol at my forehead.

"I think I'll give it to you in the head," he said. I saw his knuckles tighten around the handle.

Mutt's attention was diverted, however, by my cat that had knocked a book my mother had been reading off the bed. As Sugarfoot pounced on the book, lying now on the floor by the dresser, Mutt swung around and pointed the pistol at her. When the pistol fired, it sounded like a firecracker going off by my ear. The cat jumped straight up in the air and high-tailed it under the bed.

Mutt turned to look at me, surprise etched into his fox-like features. A thin trail of smoke was snaking out the barrel.

"There was a round in the chamber!" I cried, my ears ringing from the shot. "You cocked it while I was in the bathroom."

"Del!"

"I'm okay, Mama."

Mutt punched me in the ribs.

"Groan and moan," he said. "Act like you were hit."

"Shut up." I snatched the pistol out of his hand just before my mother burst in the room.

"Del! Are you all right?"

"Yes. Mutt was holding the gun and it went off."

Mutt was doubled up with laughter on the bed

"Is he all right?"

"Yes, he's fine. Shut up, Mutt."

"You go home, Mutt Jimson!" My mother said. "And don't you ever come back!"

Mutt jumped up and ran out of the house, and out of my life, too, for we stopped being friends after that.

I sat on the side of the bed, holding the smoking pistol in my hand.

"Oh, Del, baby, I thought you were—" My mother's lips were trembling and her face was ashen. As I looked at her I noticed, in a way I hadn't noticed before, the streaks of gray in her hair, the wrinkles around her eyes and mouth, the way her skin sagged in her throat, and I could see with a swift, cold clarity that I would lose her one day, too, although maybe not in any of the ways I had imagined. I was angry with her for this, and at myself too for my fear, and at the world for being such a dangerous place. The bees were buzzing more loudly, as if intoxicated by the fragrant wisteria. It was a smell that would linger in my memory long after we had left that house and long after I had become a man, a smell that would return during my mother's funeral service a quarter of a century later to remind me, once again, of that moment, when time seemed to pause like a hummingbird in midair, and I could hear above the delirious bees the booming of my betrayed heart.

"No need to be scared, Mama," I said, pointing at the hole in the dresser. "The bullet didn't even come close."

# Mr. Spring

Opening the door to the Pot of Gold I skate up to the bar and ask Al for a Bud draft and a shot of tequila. Then I slide onto a stool and look around to see who's there. Just old Waldo, the retired postman who drinks himself deaf and dumb every day by eight P.M., when Al sends him home in a taxi.

"Darcy, what the hell you doing on roller skates?" Al asks, as he sets the mug and shot glass on the bar.

"Celebrating spring."

Al just shakes just his head. Two weeks ago he would have made a smartass remark. But that was before I came into money.

After my inheritance, I went from being on the edge of things to the life of the party. All of a sudden people listened to what I had to say, laughed at my jokes. Even Cheryl, my girlfriend, was a lot sweeter—she actually served me breakfast in bed. But she had plenty of reasons to be nice. I bought her a whole closet full of new clothes, a VCR, a big screen TV, an exercise bike that she has yet to use, and I shared my cocaine with her. I took her daughter, Sam, shopping at the mall and bought her a roomful of toys. Sam, who is usually morose and whiny, changed, too. The night following our shopping excursion, after tucking Sam in, Cheryl came into the living room and said, "Sam wants to tell you good night."

When I went in to kiss Sam good night, she put her little arms around my neck and whispered, "Good night, Daddy."

Of course I am not her daddy, but I walked out of there feeling good all over. It's amazing the power a child can have over your heart.

I am supposed to take her shopping again this Saturday, but I can see I'll have to postpone that trip. I'll have to think of something to tell her, something else we can do. Maybe we can go roller-skating. Now there's an idea.

I rented these skates for ten dollars from a shop just down the street; that ten dollars was all the money I had left out of my inheritance. Correction: not all that's left. I still have some change. A couple of quarters, two dimes, and a nickel. But the rest of the money, ninety-two thousand dollars I inherited ten days ago from my Aunt Mary, is gone.

Where did it go?

I wrecked the MG I bought driving home from an all-night party in the country. I was coming around a curve and the MG skidded off the road, turned over a couple of times, and slammed into a tree. Luckily, I was thrown out before the car turned over the first time, and I only suffered some cuts and bruises. But the MG was totaled: my loss, since I hadn't gotten around to insuring it yet. I was using borrowed plates. The interesting thing about that accident, however, is that my life was probably saved because I wasn't wearing a seat belt. That's what the driver of the wrecker said. "If you'd have had a belt on, the car would have turned over on you. You've just got the luck of the Irish, is all I can say."

The day after I totaled my MG I bought a motorcycle, a Harley, but I loaned it to Lash McQuire. It was only supposed to be for a couple of days, but I haven't seen him since then. I heard he went to Florida. Lash is going to have some explaining to do when I see him.

I also bought a Nikon camera, which was stolen out of my car before I wrecked it. I remember giving Cheryl a big roll of cash, but she claims to have no recollection of this. Although we were both high at the time, I remember it quite clearly. We called it our rainy-day fund. I bought some new clothes, including the leather jacket I am wearing. I picked up tabs at bars and restaurants. A lot of the money went up my nose. I was partying day and night with my friends. It's no fun to do coke alone.

Ten days ago I had ninety-two thousand dollars, and today I am broke. I could let myself feel bad about this, but it's a beautiful spring day, I've got skates on my feet, and the tequila is going down as smoothly as if I was a millionaire. Tequila is a fine drink. Makes the whole world look good.

Still, there are certain things I need to consider. For example, not only am I broke, I am also unemployed. I was let go from my last job, assistant circulation manager at the newspaper. It was my responsibility to supervise all of these paperboys, which wasn't so bad. The problem was, when the paperboys didn't show up to do their routes, I had to do them. I did a few "down routes," but I overslept and let some others slide, which is why I got fired. My unemployment checks ran out around the time Aunt Mary's estate was settled. Now that my inheritance is gone, however, there are some things I need to think about. Rent, for instance. And groceries. Not to mention the electric bill, which is past due. I can't expect any help from Cheryl, either. She has no job skills other than waitressing, and lately, she hasn't even been doing much of that. Cheryl has a drinking problem, which she won't admit. God knows I've got problems, too, but the difference between Cheryl and me is I'll admit my boat has sprung a leak, and she won't. Whenever I mention her drinking to her, the first thing she says is, "Don't talk to me about drinking, not until you stop snorting cocaine."

She's got some room to talk. While I was on my roll, she was right there with me, sucking it up like a Hoover. "This is some good shit, Darcy," she'd say, her eyes watering. I wish I had a dollar for every time I heard her say that.

While we were high, we would often talk about Aunt Mary, the source of my good fortune. Actually, we didn't talk about her that much in detail, especially considering that Cheryl had never met her. What we did was thank my aunt for her generosity. I'd be in the middle of a line of pure Peruvian, and I'd look at Cheryl and say something like, "Aunt Mary was a beautiful lady, and I loved her with all my heart and soul."

"Let's dedicate this line to her," Cheryl would say. "This is some good shit."

Aunt Mary, my mother's older sister, died last year in a car accident. She was divorced, and since she'd never had children, she left her estate, consisting of her home, retirement fund, and life's savings, to my mother, my brother, and me. My brother, Alex, is starting up a mink farm with his money. He lives up in Maine with his Indian wife. I guess it was her idea to start the mink farm. Alex never liked animals much—claimed he was allergic to fur.

My mother has always predicted my brother would go far in life. "That Alex," she'd say, back in high school, "He's going to make something of himself one day. You just watch." Ever since I was a kid, my brother could do no wrong. If he made all Cs on a report card she would brag about how he made Cs without studying. But if I came home with an A on a test, my mother would want to know whose paper I'd copied.

I don't see where Alex has done so well. At twenty-nine, three years older than me, all he's managed to do that I haven't is get himself married.

A mink farm. I hope she's proud now.

Ever since I graduated from junior college, she's been on my ass for not settling down in a career. I've worked at the post office, the library; been a welder, a bartender, a truck driver, a cook, a waiter; even cleaned out stables. Trouble is, I haven't found out what I want to do with my life. "You've got to have a goal in life, Darcy," my mother says. "What's a life without purpose? A tragic waste."

I'm still trying to figure out what my purpose is, I tell her. When I do that, I'll take off like a rocket.

"I'll believe it when I see it," she says.

I am working on my second tequila when Harvey and Ray come in. They work at La Villa Grande, a restaurant here in town. Harvey is a waiter and Ray is a cook.

"What do you say, Darcy?" Harvey says.

"It's your world. I'm just passing through."

"What's with the skates?" Ray asks. "You gonna be in the roller derby?"

"They're just for fun," I say. "Because it's spring."

I ask Al to set them up with drinks, and we sit there, talking about the weather. I tell them a joke about a deaf preacher, and they both laugh. Al rolls his eyes.

An ex-linebacker for the University of Georgia, Al is still beefy, although he's got a gut now. Something about him reminds me of my old man, who dreamed of playing pro ball but ended up selling appliances for Sears. He converted our back porch into a gym and had Alex and me back there pumping iron when we were barely out of diapers. The old man bulged with muscles, which he was always getting us to feel. When I was eight he died of a massive coronary. A smoker who did no aerobic exercise, he ignored the most important muscle of all.

"Listen, you guys," I say to Harvey and Ray, "why don't you rent some skates, too, and we'll roll around town until it's time for you to go to work."

Harvey and Ray think this is a good idea. After they finish their drinks, they leave for the shop to rent their skates.

Down at the end of the bar Waldo is hunched over his beer, already getting glassy-eyed although it's barely three o'clock. He is watching the soaps on the bar's TV.

"Waldo," I say, "why don't you rent some skates and come with us?"

"Skating days behind me now, " he says.

"You should get out and live life, man," I tell him. "Age is only in your mind."

Al starts to say something but bites it back. Before my inheritance I used to come in here and bum drinks off people. I know I never left him many tips, but what the hell, I certainly treated Al right while I was on my roll. I don't see where he's got a right to have such an attitude.

I look out the window and see Harvey and Ray skate by.

I stand up, go through the motions of looking for my wallet while Al stands there, his mouth twisted into a crooked line.

"Looks like I left my wallet at home, Al. I'll have to sign the tab and pay you later."

He scowls, but hands me the pen and the tab. I sign my name, adding a ten-dollar tip for him, which I underline twice.

"Catch you next time, Al." I skate outside to see Harvey and Ray. They are laughing and swinging their arms in circles to maintain their balance.

"I did the same thing first time I put them on," I tell them. "It takes awhile to get used to them. Best thing to do is just get rolling."

We skate down the sidewalk, waving at all the people we see. We are on Oak Street, which runs into Main. The sun is shining and the trees are beginning to bud. We turn right on Main and head downtown. Ray nearly collides with a woman coming out of a store, her arms full of packages. She shouts after us as we roll on.

We pass a nun, a man selling balloons. On a bench ahead, I see three little kids, two boys and a girl.

"Where's your mama?" I ask, stopping beside them.

"In the beauty parlor," the girl says.

"We can't leave this bench," one of the boys says, wrinkling his nose.

I skate back to the balloon man, ask him how much for the balloons. A quarter each, he says. I buy three. Red, yellow, and blue. Skating back to the kids, I give each one a balloon. Their little faces light up.

"Balloons are fun," I say. "But hold on to them tight or you'll lose them. They'll float off into the sky."

The kids are looking at me as if I'm some kind of wise man. They hold their balloons tightly by the strings.

"What's your name?" the girl asks.

"I'm Mr. Spring. Now if your mama asks you where you got those balloons, you tell her Mr. Spring gave them to you."

Waving goodbye to the kids, I skate on after Harvey and Ray.

"Goodbye, Mr. Spring," they call after me. "Goodbye!"

I am now flat broke, I think, but I have just made three little kids happy with the last of my inheritance.

We skate around the block a couple of times, and then I get the idea of going down a hill for more speed. We head two blocks over to Cedar, which runs downhill to the city park.

"Let's make this a race," I suggest.

Harvey and Ray are both up for it.

At the top of the hill we skate out into the street. We stand there, looking down. I feel as if I am about to embark on some momentous journey.

I look at Harvey, then Ray. "On the count of three."

They both nod.

"One, two, three!"

We take off down the hill. I crouch down, moving ahead of Harvey. But Ray keeps up with me. Behind us a car honks, then speeds around us, the driver shaking his fist out the window.

I flash him the bird.

The sky is full of golden light. The skates make a sound like music. The wind sings in my ears. Crouching down on the skates, I edge ahead of Ray. The road downhill is wide open. As I raise my fist in victory, I realize I have found my place: it is in this perfect moment, a whole shimmering world of which I am the glorious and eternal king.

# Specks of Gold

Driving into Bayside, Thomas tried to picture Julie's face and found he could not recall her clearly. She was as hazy as a water-caught moon. How can that be? he wondered. His chest felt tight and his head ached. How can that be?

He found the funeral parlor on a side street near the courthouse. He drove slowly past it, studying the windows, noting the other buildings on the block: a gas station, a warehouse, apartments. Remembering Julie's step-father's abusive manner on the telephone, he experienced a sudden attack of anxiety. He's the law in this town, he thought. It's not too late to leave.

But he couldn't forget his promise to Julie. His heart pounding, he parked his truck and studied his map. He had driven into Bayside on Highway 17, which became Main Street inside the town limits. The highway continued east to the next town, Navissa, and then on to the Rastahock Sound. The Indian River flowed four miles south of Bayside, curved around its eastern side, and continued east toward the sound. Beyond were the barrier islands and then the sea.

He drove back up Main Street, passing a pool hall, a flower shop, a pawnshop, a drug store. He vaguely remembered Julie's telling him something about that drugstore. What was it?

The town's two motels had no vacancies. A clerk at the second motel he visited explained that the rooms were filled due to a coin show a state numismatic association held in Bayside every fall. The clerk suggested he try Mrs. Grantly's boarding house—on a side street a few blocks east of the courthouse.

The boarding house was white with green shutters. Three old men sat on the porch, two of them playing chess. The one sitting alone looked at

Thomas through thick glasses. He had a hook where his left hand should have been.

"Is Mrs. Grantly here?" Thomas asked.

"I reckon she is. Why do you ask?"

"I'd like to rent a room."

"Why didn't you say so?" The old man got up from the chair, farting like a tuba, and went into the house.

While Thomas waited the chess players cast him furtive glances. He realized that he might appear eccentric—a man wearing a fedora and driving a truck. The fedora, which he had found in a second-hand store, had been part of a costume he had worn on his first date with Julie. They had gone to a costume party, Thomas as a 1930s detective, Julie as Amelia Earhart.

Soon the front door opened and a tall, broad-shouldered woman with gray hair came out, followed by the old man. Thomas took off his fedora. Introducing himself as Adam Harrell, he asked if she had a room for rent.

"Are you here for the coin show?" the woman asked. Her eyes behind her glasses were a peculiar shade of bronze.

"No, ma'am. Just passing through."

"Is that your truck?"

"Yes, ma'am."

"What are you planning to do with that straw?"

"Guess I'll have to sleep in it if I can't find a room."

The woman did not return his smile. "How long do you need the room for?"

"One night."

"I usually rent rooms by the week. But I do have one room available. It'll be twenty-five dollars, in advance."

He took out his wallet and paid her the money.

Mrs. Grantly waited on the porch while he got his suitcase out of the truck. When he came back she told him she would show him to his room. He stepped into a long hallway that smelled of pine disinfectant. The flight of stairs at the end of the hall creaked as they ascended.

The room was off the hallway at the top of the stairs. It was furnished with a narrow bed, a nightstand, a chair, and dresser. There was a Bible on the nightstand.

Mrs. Grantly told him the bathroom was across the hall and that he would find a towel and washcloth in the top drawer of his dresser. "We have certain rules which everyone is expected to follow," she added. "No loud noises or radios, no guests, and lights out by eleven P.M. And absolutely no use of alcohol or use of drugs. Is that clear?"

"Yes, ma'am." Thomas closed the door and sat on the bed, listening to her footsteps on the stairs. He opened the suitcase, took out a bottle of whiskey and a tumbler, and poured himself a drink. His hands were trembling. He hadn't been sleeping well since his conversation with Julie's mother, Mrs. Lawrence, two days earlier. He had called to tell her that Julie wanted her body to be cremated, the ashes buried at sea. Julie's mother had been sympathetic but confused. "I don't know what to do now," she had said. "The funeral arrangements have already been made."

"Couldn't you change them?" Thomas had asked.

"Yes," she said slowly. "I suppose that's what we'll have to do."

At that point, however, Mrs. Lawrence's husband—Julie's stepfather— had broken in. Thomas heard them arguing, then the stepfather took the phone. "This is Buck Lawrence. Who am I speaking to?"

"Thomas Miller."

"I got news for you, Mr. Thomas Miller, that girl is gonna receive a decent Christian burial."

"She wanted to be cremated, Mr. Lawrence. She felt—"

"I don't give a damn what she wanted!" Buck Lawrence hung up before Thomas could ask to speak to Julie's mother.

Thomas had gotten the names and numbers of the town's three funeral homes from information. A man at the second one he called told him a driver was due in with Julie's body that evening. She was to be buried on Thursday, two days away. There would be a memorial service at the chapel in the funeral home.

He sat on the bed, trying to visualize Julie, but all he could think about was his promise to her. They were discussing their fears, and Julie revealed that her greatest fear was being buried alive. "That's why I want to be cremated when I die, Tom." What did he say? Something like, "There shouldn't be any problem with that."

That night she had wakened him, crying. "I dreamed I was buried in the ground." She clung to him, her body trembling. "Thomas, if I die promise me you won't let them put me in the ground. I want to be cremated and my ashes spread in the sea."

"I promise." It had been an easy enough thing to say. "Now go back to sleep."

"Do you promise, really?" He could feel her heart beating against his hand.

"Yes," he said. "I promise."

Not long after this conversation, Thomas and Julie's relationship ran aground. After a series of missed cues, foolish blunders, and general misfortunes in the arena of love, Thomas thought he had finally mastered the art of enjoying a woman's company without giving his heart in the process, but Julie—sweet, vulnerable Julie—had broken down his defenses. When he realized he had fallen for her he panicked and bailed out, telling her only that he wasn't ready to be tied down to one woman. An unfortunate choice of words, for Julie responded with, "What do you think I am—a hitching post?" Their last evening together was deeply painful for Thomas. Julie said little, but her quiet tears scalded his heart. Thomas, who was often mystified by his emotions where women he loved were concerned, told himself their separation was temporary—a hiatus to allow him time to get his fears under control. He even started seeing a therapist.

But a month after their breakup, Julie had died of a cocaine overdose. She injected the cocaine at a party, not while she was alone, Thomas thought. She was surrounded by people. But Julie had been off drugs two years when he met her, and he couldn't shake the guilt—the lingering notion he had caused her death.

The last time he had seen her he had been talking to a woman at the Blue Knight, a bar he often visited when he wasn't working as a surveyor. Thomas wasn't dating the woman, but when Julie saw them together she looked hurt, and she left immediately afterwards. Thomas hurried out to the parking lot, wanting to tell her that the woman was just an acquaintance, but Julie was already gone.

Ever since they had broken up, he hadn't been able to get her out of his mind. He still slept in the flannel shirt she had given him for his birthday. And he kept another gift from her on the nightstand beside his bed — a rock with a face painted on it and an inscription below: *Everybody needs somebody. My somebody is you.*

The river curved around the town like a crescent; he saw the shape of it on the map.

He followed Main Street east out of town, crossing the bridge over the river. Just past the bridge on his right there was a marina and, beyond the marina, a small restaurant, Cap'n Jack's. He drove on to Navissa, eight miles from Bayside. Four miles past Navissa, still on Highway 17, he crossed the bridge that spanned Indian River Sound and connected the mainland to the barrier islands. This was the simplest route to the sea.

He returned to Bayside and tried the second route, heading west on Main. A mile past the gas station he had stopped at on his way into town, he turned left onto Marsh Road. Two miles south, just past a wooden bridge, he turned left onto Seaview, which crossed the Indian River and went all the way to the sound. Although the second route was longer than the first, it was more private and it circumvented Navissa.

That's the best way to go, Thomas thought.

He ate supper at Cap'n Jack's after the sun had gone down. He could barely taste his food. A jukebox in the corner played songs by Merle Haggard, George Jones. His waitress wore a red rose in her hair. She smiled a lot and seemed concerned that he didn't finish his meal.

Outside, he got a flashlight from his truck and walked across the road to the river. He sat on an outcropping of rock and watched the cars crossing the bridge. He aimed the flashlight at the water, illuminating scraps of silver on the surface: dead fish. He wondered if there were a plant close by that pumped chemicals into the river. Or maybe the fish had just given up and died because they were tired of being fish. The waitress had seemed lonely. Perhaps he should have struck up a conversation with her. She might have met him somewhere for a drink after her shift. She would probably live in a trailer or a small house, with a couple of children she was raising alone. After telling him her life's story, a tale of misery and betrayal, she would reward them both with a friendly lay. In the morning he would forget his crazy scheme and make this trip to Bayside a simple exercise in nostalgia, a visit to the funeral of a former girlfriend. There would be the customary rituals: the eulogy, the ride to the cemetery, a few shopworn phrases mouthed over the coffin, the interment. And he would be back in Durham by dark, in time to catch the band playing at the Blue Knight.

"That's what I ought to do all right," he said, and he skipped a rock over the surface of the river.

He lay on the bed, trying to sleep. Doors opened, closed. A toilet flushed. He heard someone say, ". . . a beautiful MS sixty-five, only ten percent above the price of gold." He got up and went down the stairs, out to the front porch. The chess players were seated at a small table, leaning over the board, sucking their pipe stems like nipples in their toothless mouths. Thomas sat in a chair and watched them. When the game was over, the winner invited him to play.

"No, thanks. I'm not very good at chess."

"Tough game to master." The speaker's sideburns were so long they resembled whiskers.

"We'd play cards," said the other man," but she don't 'low it."

"Did you see her husband?" the one with sideburns asked. "The one with the missing hand?"

"That's her husband?"

"Aye. Every afternoon he waits for the trains to come by." The man tapped the side of his head. "Train don't run anywhere near here."

"He used to work for the railroad," the other man said.

"She hates to hear him talk about the train. If it was me I'd let him talk. Can't see no harm in it."

"She runs a tight ship. Last night she came up and made me turn off the light. Wasn't three minutes past eleven."

"I hear she—" the man with the sideburns hushed as the front door opened. Mrs. Grantly came out and sat down in a rocker.

The old men began setting up the board for another game. The only sound was the squeaking of Mrs. Grantly's rocking chair.

Thomas woke up suddenly. He had dozed off waiting for the coin collectors in the next room to fall asleep. They had stayed up past midnight, talking. He got up and put on his shoes and coat. Picking up the suitcase, he opened the door and stepped into the hall. The stairs creaked as he descended. He stopped, silently cursing the coin collectors who had hit the town like a plague of locusts. He went on more slowly, staying close to the wall. As he was tiptoeing down the hall, the suitcase struck a stand, nearly knocking an urn to the floor. He stopped, expecting Mrs. Grantly to appear and demand, "Young man, where are you going at this hour?"

He unlocked the front door and hurried down the steps to his truck, throwing the suitcase inside. The sky was cloudy with only a few stars visible. He put the truck in neutral and began pushing it down the street. Past the house, he jumped in the truck and started up the engine. He drove the route he had mapped out earlier, taking back streets to the funeral parlor. He got his bag of tools from under the seat and put it on the floor. He knew the police might be able to identify him later, but by then he would have accomplished his purpose. He tried not to think about what might happen to him if he were caught. I'll worry about that when the time comes, he thought. He had already decided he was willing to go to jail in order keep his promise. A jail term would end at some point, but his unfulfilled promise to Julie would haunt him the rest of his life.

He was getting ready to turn into the parking lot behind the funeral parlor when he saw the police car parked at the gas station across the street. Damn! He kept going straight. As he turned on to Main, he checked the mirror; the police car was following him. He pushed his bag of tools under the seat.

The blue light began flashing. Thomas pulled over and got out his driver's license and registration card. He rolled down the window and waited.

The flashlight blinded him. "Could I see your license and registration?" Thomas handed him his driver's license and registration card.

"What are you doing in Bayside, Mr. Miller?"

"I'm with the coin show. Had a little trouble sleeping so I thought I'd go for a ride."

"Where you staying?"

"Mrs. Grantly's boarding house."

"Why'd you bring your suitcase?"

"I've got some valuable coins. I was afraid someone might steal them."

"What's the straw for?"

"My horse." Thomas's voice cracked.

"You'd best go on back to Mrs. Grantly's. We don't like strangers cruising the streets at night here."

The policeman followed Thomas back to the boarding house. His heart was racing. It was clear he couldn't get her out now.

Dammit, I tried, he thought, as he climbed the stairs to his room. He stood at the window looking out at the sky. The moon was a circle of silver light behind the clouds.

"Bad-luck time," he said. His arms and legs felt as if they had weights strapped to them. "Bad luck all around."

He woke up to the sounds of a flushing toilet, creaking stairs, voices. It was morning. His face touched something cold: the empty whiskey bottle. His eyeballs ached, and his few hours of whiskey sleep had been plagued by bad dreams. In one dream he had been trying to rescue a child trapped in a cave. He had crawled for what seemed like hours through twisted tunnels, hearing its cries but unable to find it.

The rock Julie had given him was on the stand by his bed. He picked it up and pressed it to his lips. "Julie," he said. Tears filled his eyes. "Julie, Julie, Julie . . ."

He showered, put on clean clothes, and sat at the chair at the desk. He was sweating and his head hurt. The funeral service was to begin at one P.M. He figured they would be putting Julie's coffin into the hearse around two o'clock. I'll have to do it then, he thought.

He picked up his coat and felt the sticks of dynamite hidden in the lining. He had bought the dynamite three months earlier from a hitchhiker named Adam Harrell, who was carrying it in a backpack. The hitchhiker told Thomas he had stolen the dynamite from a construction company he had worked for. "They laid a bunch of us off with no warning and cheated me out of a week's pay," he said. "I took this to even the score." Thomas had no particular purpose in mind for the dynamite when he bought it, five sticks for twenty dollars. He had mostly just wanted to help the man out.

Thomas studied his face in the mirror over the dresser. He didn't look well. Grinning a lopsided grin, he said, "Sincerity failed, Julie. Stealth failed. All that's left now is bold action."

He lay down on the bed and tried to relax.

Heavy footsteps on the stairs. Something about them increased his anxiety.

The door to his room opened suddenly, and a solidly built man in a dark gray suit stepped in. He had a thick neck and a crew cut. Behind him stood a uniformed policeman.

"Ever hear of knocking?" Thomas asked.

The man jerked his coat back to reveal a gold badge pinned to his shirt. "I'm Buck Lawrence, chief of police in Bayside."

"Howdy, Buck."

"You don't have to tell me who you are." The chief jabbed a thick finger at Thomas. "On account of I already know."

"I know a little bit about you, too." Thomas smiled, but only with his lips. He remembered Julie telling him about running away from home once after Buck beat her with an electrical cord.

"Hear you went for a little ride last night."

"That could be."

"Why'd you do that, wonder?"

"Must've been restless."

"Uh-huh." The chief looked around the room, nodding his head. "I've been in police work for twenty-two years, and during that time I've developed an eye for human trash. Once I spot that type of person I don't pay much attention to anything he says on account of I know it's just so much rat shit."

"Gift like that must come in handy in your line of work."

"You haul your sorry ass out of town the minute she's in the ground, you hear?"

"Hadn't planned on staying around."

"That's a wise choice. We don't need you in this town, boy. We don't want you here. Now, do we understand each other?"

"I think we have a perfect understanding," Thomas said.

Buck Lawrence turned and left, the uniformed cop following him like a shadow.

The chief's cologne lingered in the room, musky and sickeningly sweet. Thomas got up and opened the window. He had a nervous tic in his eye. He wondered if the chief had noticed it. He got out a pen and piece of paper and wrote the chief a note: *Dear Buck, Prometheus stole fire from the gods and gave it to man so that he, too, could become god-like.*

He left the note sticking out of the Bible on the stand beside the bed, figuring Mrs. Grantly would find it and give it to him.

Thomas stood in the parking lot behind the funeral parlor and watched the pallbearers carry Julie's coffin out the back door and down the walkway. Black-clad people walked by him to their cars. The pallbearers were loading the coffin into the back of the hearse. The keys were still in the ignition.

The light was the cold, eerie kind that comes from an acetylene torch— it burns away all the shadows, making things stand out with a clarity so intense it's dreamlike. It's a light stripped of all mercy, Thomas thought.

He lit a cigar and walked toward the black gleaming hearse. Stopping near the door to the driver's seat, he listened to a man give the chauffeur directions on the route to the cemetery. The chief was on the front lawn, politicking among a group of men.

Thomas opened the door and slid into the driver's seat, quickly locking the doors. The engine turned over and over, without starting. Someone shouted and pounded on the window. Thomas bit down on the cigar and watched the chief slowly turn his head in the direction of the hearse. There was the red face, the gash of a mouth, the eyes that would bug out when he saw what Thomas was doing.

The engine fired. Thomas shifted into drive and pushed the accelerator down. As the hearse shot forward Thomas managed to flash the chief a grin and a salute.

He heard more shouting behind him, but he couldn't tell if it was the chief or not. He sped down Main Street, the hearse already going so fast it was like riding a thunderbolt. He ran a stoplight, passed a car, a truck. Soon he could hear the sirens.

He saw a police car in the rearview mirror—two others following behind. The chief would be in the first one. Thomas sensed a psychic connection between himself and the chief; he imagined he knew what the chief was thinking: How can he expect to get away with this? I'll run him off the road, right into a goddamned tree. And he'll be dead meat, then. Dead meat.

146

A curve ahead and a semi. Too late to slow down now. He hit the horn and swerved into the lane for oncoming traffic, passing the truck in the curve. A long blast from the semi's horn. Luck was with him—no traffic in the oncoming lane. But coming out of the curve he lost control of the hearse and careened onto the shoulder of the road. He got the hearse back on the road, then checked the mirror. A police car passed the truck, siren screaming. They were on a straight section of the highway now, the car in front gaining on him.

Tires squealing, he turned left onto Marsh Road. One of the police cars overshot the turn, but the other two stayed with him.

He took a stick of dynamite from the lining of his coat, then rolled down the window. He could see the police car in the rearview mirror. Thomas puffed on the cigar; he touched the red ember to the fuse and dropped the hissing dynamite out the window.

*Kerboooooooooom*!

When he looked back the police car was in a cornfield. The other cars were slowing down. Thomas felt lightheaded but resolute. He sent the chief a thought-message: Stay back, Buck, if you know what's good for you.

He saw the wooden bridge ahead and eased off the accelerator. Just past the bridge he pulled onto the side of the road. Leaving the engine running, he got out of the hearse and slid down the bank into the icy stream. He waded under the bridge and, using electrician's tape, he attached two sticks of dynamite to one of the supporting beams. He lit the fuses with the cigar, then scrambled toward the bank.

The dynamite exploded just as he rolled behind a pine, hurling debris past the tree. His ears ringing, he walked back to the road to look at the damage. The bridge was down. Beams and debris strewn in the creek and along the road. The air sour with the ammonium nitrate residue.

On down the road he could see the police cars coming. Sly bastards had turned off their sirens.

He tossed the cigar into the creek and got back into the hearse.

A couple of hundred yards past the bridge he stopped again and picked up the five-gallon can of gasoline he had hidden in the weeds. He put the gasoline can in the back of the hearse next to the coffin. He sat in the driver's seat and rested his forehead against the steering wheel. To calm himself he composed a mental note to Julie: Dear Julie, Sorry I let you down. I wish we could have worked it out. I was scared, I guess. What a weird little place Bayside is. A town full of bats. Love, Thomas.

He noticed the hearse had a radio. He turned the dial and found a gospel station. The Tuscaloosa Choir was singing, "Ain't No Excuse for Not Serving the Lord." He turned left onto the road that ran east toward the sea. Farmland on either side, then a long stretch of woods, then a swamp filled with cypress. He sang along with the songs on the radio, keeping time with his palm against the steering wheel. Crossing the bridge over Indian River, he looked down at the water. Maybe I should put her there, he thought. But Julie's face appeared in his memory, holding him to his promise to bury her ashes at sea. He could recall her quite clearly now—her nose, her lips, the shape of her face. Her eyes were gray, with specks of gold. More memories of Julie spilled out of the trunk in his memory where they had been locked. He remembered the spicy scent of her hair, the feeling of her body against his at night. And he remembered what she had told him about the drugstore: she had gotten her first real job there, making ice cream sundaes behind the counter. His memory of her now seemed more real than the shabby little town she was from.

When he reached the sound, he stopped and looked both ways for road-blocks, police cars. None in sight. He turned left and continued north toward the turnoff to the bridge. He had apparently eluded his pursuers.

He drove across the bridge spanning the sound. Sunlight shimmered on the water below. He had the sensation of having made this journey before, perhaps in some dream. He took the first access road to the beach and followed the winding road past sand dunes, beach grass, and shrubs to another road that ran parallel to the shore. He turned onto this road and drove past beach houses and cottages. A man sitting on a porch turned to watch the hearse go by. The sea was green and shining beyond the dune line, the sky a bold, glittering blue. The beach houses and cottages became less frequent until finally there were just the dunes, the beach grass, and the sea. He passed a pile of concrete slabs—the broken vertebrae of an earlier section of highway the state had moved inland to escape the invading surf. Beyond the slabs he saw a path leading to the beach. He turned onto the path, gunning the engine to keep from getting stuck in the sand. The momentum carried him down to the sea's edge. The beach was empty except for the sea birds— sandpipers, terns, and gulls.

He went around to the back of the hearse, opened the door, and climbed in. Lifting the lid from the coffin, he knelt beside Julie. She wore a white dress; her face looked strange with all the makeup. He walked down to the sea and, scooping up some water in his hands, he went back to her and cleaned her face with his fingers. He took one of her hands in his and rested his head on the coffin. "It'll be all right now," he said. "There's nothing to be afraid of."

He kissed her forehead and poured the gasoline over her, using the last of it to drench his fedora. He climbed out of the hearse, lit the fedora with a match and tossed it into the coffin—then turned and ran for the dunes.

He sat on a dune and watched the hearse explode in a fireball, a thick black plume of smoke rising into the sky. He put his hand in his pocket, curling his fingers around the rock she had given him. It was round and smooth as a heart. "Goodbye, Julie," he said.

A flock of pelicans flew by, turning their heads in perfect unison to look back at the flaming hearse. Thomas waved to them as they passed.

# Violets

You are a passenger in a car on the outskirts of a small, Southern city. Looking out the window you see a woman with a green scarf around her neck, kneeling by an embankment covered with wild violets. You have no way of knowing, from your viewpoint in the moving car, the conversation that took place minutes earlier in the flower shop nearby. You did not hear the bell over the door jingle as the woman entered, nor did you see the clerk look up and flinch when he saw her face. It looked as if it had been taken apart and pieced back together, with the connecting seams only partially hidden by makeup. Her nose was off-center and misshapen; her right eye an inch higher than its companion, which looked off to the side. The high one, clear and sky-blue, gazed steadily at the clerk.

"Yes, ma'am. Can I help you?"

"I'd like to buy some flowers."

"What type of arrangement were you thinking of?"

"Something simple."

"We have some lovely samples on display on the table over there. From fifteen dollars on up."

The table was several yards to her right. She walked over to look at the display. A slender woman with chestnut hair, moving gracefully, her head tilted down as if in prayer.

She returned to the counter. "I don't see anything there that feels quite right. Can I buy some individual flowers in a vase?"

"How about long-stemmed roses? They're six dollars apiece, including the vase. Thirty-two-fifty for half a dozen."

"No. Not roses."

"Is it a special occasion?"

"The occasion? I don't even know where to begin." She shifted her gaze to the wall behind the clerk. "She was driving a nineteen seventy-one Cadillac. No seat belts, of course. It was a gaudy purple and it always reeked of her perfume. Regina never had any taste."

"It's all right," he said. "You don't need to explain."

"Yes, I do." She looked back at the clerk. "Did you know that I once got rid of all the mirrors in my house?"

"No, ma'am."

"But I couldn't banish reflections. You can see your image in a spoon, a windowpane, a pool of water, even someone's eyes. Did you know I could see myself in your expression when you first looked at me?"

"Really, I—"

"Don't worry. I'm used to people's reactions. I've had to get used to them. You should have seen me before the surgeons did their work. I've had twenty-five operations since I was twelve. And during all that time, do you think she ever came to see me? Or bothered to call and find out how I was doing? I did receive a get-well card. Unsigned. Only way I knew it was from her was I could smell her horrible perfume on it. Regina was probably drunk when she sent that card."

"Who's Regina?"

"She used to be my stepmother. My father divorced her."

"You want the flowers for her?"

"Yes. She's in the hospital. Dying of cancer."

"Let me show you our catalogue of special arrangements." He opened the booklet and set it on the counter in front of her. But she hardly looked at them.

"I remember how fast she was driving that night, the way she was taking curves on that slick highway, rain slamming into the car like bullets. I was scared to death. I begged her to slow down, but she might as well have been deaf. She was all pumped full of booze and beyond caring about anything, especially not a frightened twelve-year-old girl. Regina always loved living on the edge. And she was a master at wiggling out of consequences.

'I was drunk,' she'd say, as if that could provide her with an ironclad excuse for any failure, any cruelty."

The woman's eye was fixed again on the wall behind him, where a clock hung. When the shop was quiet like this, the clerk could hear the clock ticking.

"Where were you going—in the car?" he asked.

"To a piano recital. My father was supposed to take me, but at the last minute he called to say he had to stay late at work. He asked Regina to drive me there—he didn't know how drunk she was. There was someone else scheduled to perform before me, and he promised to be there by the time I started playing. But I never got to play. On the way there she took a curve too fast and we crashed into a tree. Regina wasn't hurt that seriously. A broken arm, some bruises. A fractured pelvis. But I went through the windshield. My own father didn't even recognize me when he saw me in the emergency room."

The clerk swallowed, his larynx moving up and down in his slender neck. He had a small shaving cut on his chin.

"Regina not only destroyed my childhood, she also left me with this—" she touched her face with her fingers. "You can't imagine the anger I've felt, the tortures I've dreamed. I used to picture her fingernails being pulled off one by one, her skin burned with hot pokers."

The clerk's eyes were wide and shining. He looked like a child listening to a ghost story.

"But hatred is like acid. It can eat you away until there's nothing left inside. I've learned things, you know. It isn't like I haven't had plenty of time to think. For years I only considered Regina in terms of what she did to me. Only recently was I able to consider that there may be another way to see her. As someone lost and alone, for instance. Someone dying without love."

"Perhaps a custom arrangement is what you need. I'll go back and talk to the manager."

But the clerk didn't move.

The woman was looking out the window. The embankment along the highway was abloom with violets.

"Look at those violets. I don't know why I didn't think of them."

"You want to take her violets?"

"I passed them on the way in and didn't even see them."

"They certainly wouldn't cost anything."

"That's not the point." She looked quickly back at him, and he could see the curved image of his own face in her sky-blue eye.

"Of course not." He tilted his head back so he could no longer see his image in her eye. "I think you should do what feels right."

"I'm glad you understand that. Thank you so much for listening."

"No problem. I hope everything works out okay."

"I just need to do this one simple thing. Pay her a visit, wish her well. And give her those violets."

She pushed open the door and went outside. Through the glass he watched her walk out to the embankment, kneel down, and begin picking the violets.

But he is not the only one who observes her. At this point you pass by in a car and see a woman with a green scarf around her neck, kneeling in a galaxy of violets. You cannot see her scarred, disfigured face. She is just a momentary image in the endless stream of things you see from a moving car—of no more significance than men framing a house, a family eating at a picnic table, or a girl riding a horse across a sunlit meadow, her hair flowing behind her in the wind.

# Astronauts

Vicky, a woman I shot pool with, told me about the job at the detox house. They needed a night man, she said. "It's working with drunks and crazies—you'll fit right in." I had plenty of experience as a drunk, and I was used to being up at night. Also, I was unemployed, my refrigerator was nearly empty, and I was two months behind on my rent.

The detox house was a white frame house on Southern Avenue, next to an all-night pizza parlor. I rode my bike over there from my house on East Elm on a spring morning when the trees were just beginning to bud and the city was bathed with a fine, gold light. A coffee-colored woman answered the door. A pink scar curved around from her right eye to the corner of her mouth.

I asked to speak to the manager. She said, "Wait here."

A slim brunette came to the door. "You want to see me?"

"Yes, ma'am. I'm Josh Nichols. Heard you were looking for help with the night shift."

"Do you have any experience working with drunks?"

"Used to be one."

"It didn't hurt your looks," she said, and she invited me in.

The front room of the detox house was an office that looked like it had once been a porch. There was a couch to my left, a desk to the right. Through the top glass section of a door I could see the woman who had answered the door and two sallow-faced men sitting on a couch, watching TV. The detox house manager, who introduced herself as Ursa Schmidt, interviewed me at the desk. She had intense black eyes, a pageboy haircut, and a nervous animal energy that reminded me of a thoroughbred racehorse. She wanted to know how long I had been dry.

"About six months," I lied. Actually, it had been less than three.

"Did you quit with the help of AA?"

"No, ma'am. Just cold turkey."

"Very good. That shows a strong will."

"At the time I didn't feel like I had much of a choice."

"We drunks always have a choice. It's a daily battle, too. Booze is like Satan himself—seductive, cunning, and very powerful."

"Interesting way to put it," I said.

She gave me an application to fill out. For references I put down the names of my doctor, a woman I used to work with at the university in town, and a former music professor I hoped would still remember me.

"I'll check your references and give you a call," the manager said.

As I left on my bike I was thinking I should have better references. My doctor, a Cuban, spoke with a heavy accent, and although he had cured me of the clap twice, I wasn't sure he would remember me well enough to recommend me for a job. My co-worker at the university had not been my supervisor; she was also aware I had been fired. I hadn't seen my former professor in more than three years. With all of this in mind, I resisted the urge to go down to Harry's Bar and order a shot of tequila. Instead I headed back to my house, planning to give the place a spring cleaning. When I got there I found an eviction notice in my mailbox.

I went into the living room and sat on my bed. Paint was peeling off the walls, the hot water heater was broken, the floors were bowed in the center, and the furnace hadn't worked since Valentine's Day. The landlord always acted like I was asking for a pint of blood every time I asked him to fix something. "Rachel," I said, looking up at the mannequin beside my bed. "Looks like we have to find another place to live."

The mannequin's face was turned toward the doorway, her hand raised as if beckoning someone to come in. I stole her one drunken night from a boutique on East Main—smashed the window with a brick and took her off under my arm. I used to buy clothes for her, dress her in different outfits. No telling how much money I blew on Rachel's wardrobe. Silk dresses, scarves, shoes, gloves, even jewelry. I stole her a few weeks after I broke up with my wife, Iris. We'd been high school sweethearts, together since we were seventeen, married our senior year in college. At twenty-eight, we had a decent brick home, new Volvos, and we were talking about having kids. I managed the student cafeteria at the university in town, and Iris owned a successful dance studio. Then I found out she was sleeping with a mechanic at the dealership where she got her car serviced. The way I found out was, the guy's wife called me and told me about it. She even came over to my house with evidence: a fuzzy but incriminating photo of Iris and her husband together in bed. Her sister had taken it through a window. She had a magnifying glass to help me see the sordid details more clearly. It was Iris all right. My sweet wife, Iris. Bestowing her favors on the guy who changed the oil in her car. A man with greasy hair and a tattoo of a spider web on his bicep. A man with two kids and a wife who had been crying so much her eyes were red and swollen. Her mascara had run, and she looked like a sad little clown.

After Iris and I broke up, I went downhill fast, turned my anger in on myself, let booze take over my life. I got fired from my job at the university, wrecked my car, and lost my driver's license for DWI. I ran through my savings and my share of equity in our home. I got a job playing sax with the Zombies, a local rock band, but we fell to arguing among ourselves and ended up going our separate ways. I can't even remember what we were fighting about. The year and a half after my marriage ended was like a long, bad dream. It's as if that time were just missing from my life, in the same way that Iris was gone.

I woke up one morning with a stranger in my bed. A monstrously fat woman. She was so fat she looked like she had escaped from a freak show. If she rolled over on me, I was road kill. I had no idea how she had gotten there, couldn't remember meeting her, bringing her home. My brain was fried. I had the shakes bad. I sat up and looked around my living room—at the pizza boxes, whiskey bottles, and beer cans strewn all over the floor— and realized my whole life was dangling from a frayed rope. That was the day I stopped drinking and using drugs. Wouldn't even drink a cold beer. None of my friends could believe it.

Vicky let me move in with her, but she established some ground rules first. She would cover my share of the rent and utilities until I got my first paycheck from the detox house, but she expected to be repaid. I would have to help with cooking and cleaning, too. Also, she didn't eat meat and wasn't particularly fond of it being cooked in the kitchen. And Rachel had to go in the basement. I wasn't happy about that, but what choice did I have? It was either that or I was out on the street.

Vicky is from Texas. She's almost six feet tall, has straight, naturally blonde hair and gray blue eyes that remind me of some Norse sea her ancestors probably crossed in order to rape and pillage residents of coastal villages. She moved to this town with her drug-dealing boyfriend a few years back, and after he went to prison, she got a job waiting tables at the Sunshine Kitchen, a vegetarian restaurant. She came home nights smelling of herbs and spices and freshly baked bread. To look at her, you would never know she had ever put an unwholesome thing in her body. With her pollen-colored hair, ivory skin, and long, toned legs, she looked like a poster girl for good health.

Vicky's boyfriend beat her up a couple of times before he got busted by the feds, and he hurt her in other ways, too. But we didn't talk about that. No sense in swimming in the dirty water that's already run under the bridge.

"The night shift is the hardest one," Jasmine said, during one of my orientation sessions. Jasmine, who had answered the door on my first visit, was the only staff member who was not a recovering alcoholic. But she had been married to a drunk, according to Ursa. That's how she got the scar on her face. Her ex-husband had done it with a broken bottle.

"Why is it so hard?"

"Drunks just get crazier at night," Jasmine said. She added that her husband used to go after her during the full moon. "I still get the heebie-jeebies every time the moon is full." She said after he slashed her face with the bottle she had planned to kill him because she knew that was the only way she would ever get away from him, but with the help of her minister, her church family, and a battered women's shelter, she had finally been able to get away from him for good.

"I thank God I never did it," Jasmine said. "Then I'd have his blood on my soul. Now all I've got is his mark on my face. I still have to think about him, though, every time I look in the mirror."

"It's not that bad," I told her. "Besides, you've got beautiful eyes. That's what people are going to notice, not some little scar."

"It's not so little, but that's a sweet thing to say. Watch out for Ursa, concentrate on helping these poor folk, and you'll do fine here. It's not such a bad job."

Before Ursa let me work the night shift, she assigned me to work a week of daytime orientation sessions. This gave me the opportunity to meet the staff and the drunks and to gain an understanding of how the house operated. In addition to the front office and living room, there was a kitchen, bathroom, and three bedrooms. The largest bedroom had two beds, so the house could accommodate five residents at once. It usually took about five days for a resident to dry all the way out. Ursa seemed proud that the detox house did not rely on drugs. "We're all natural here," she said. "Just good food, tea, orange juice, coffee, and plenty of rest."

The daytime staff members were glad to see me. They had been taking turns pulling the night shift since someone named Blackie had quit on short notice. Even before I worked a night shift, I could see why it would be challenging. At least two staff members were on duty at all times during the day, but the night person worked alone. And like Jasmine had said, a person with a troubled mind just has a harder time at night. Which might be related to a time when human beings lived in caves and had to worry about pythons and saber-toothed tigers dropping out of trees.

I was beginning to see why I had gotten the job with such dubious references.

The residents, as Ursa referred to them, were tense and jittery, especially after the booze started wearing off. Sometimes they would break into hellacious sweats that made them look like they were in a sauna. It was up to the staff members to feed them, keep them calm, counsel them about the twelve steps of AA, listen to them talk, and be on hand in case trouble developed. Trouble could take many different forms, according to Ursa, including fights, suicide attempts, withdrawal seizures, diabetic coma, and an attack on a staff member. One of the biggest dangers was DTs, or delirium tremens. She said drunks who experienced seizures could sustain head injuries and broken bones from slamming into things. They could also choke to death on their own tongues.

"How can I tell someone is going into DTs?"

"You'll know, don't worry," she said. "You must call the rescue squad immediately. We don't want any dead bodies here. Some fool wants to die, he can pull that trick somewhere else."

"Sure hope nothing like that happens on my watch."

"Anything can happen when you're dealing with drunks. We're all — how do you Southerners say it? — batshit crazy." Ursa laughed a big, booming laugh, but I failed to see any humor in the subject.

My first two nights solo weren't that bad, but my third night I sat up until five A.M. with a resident who thought he had spiders crawling on him. I spent hours trying to convince him there weren't any spiders. By the time he finally ran out of steam and fell asleep, I imagined I was seeing them, too.

After I started working the night shift, Vicky and I didn't see each other much during the week. When I would get home I could only sleep a few hours before the sun woke me up. Vicky put some black plastic over the blinds to help. Even in the dark room, however, I still couldn't sleep much past one P.M. Vicky was patient with me when I was cranky and nervous due to lack of sleep. She complimented me for having the discipline to work nights, she listened with interest when I told her about little ways I felt I had helped the patients, and she was especially pleased when I turned my first paycheck over to her.

For some reason, however, Vicky had taken a dislike to Ursa. She called her the Fraulein.

"Why don't you like Ursa?" I asked. "You've never even met her."

"Intuition," Vicky said, tapping her temple.

A retired Army officer worked the weekend night shift, giving me two nights off. Saturday night Vicky and I would go out dancing or to the pool hall, two of her favorite pastimes. She had this way of bending over a pool table, her shapely buttocks jutting up at a jaunty angle, and sighting down the cue stick with a smoky blue eye framed by a cascade of blonde hair that made my chest tighten up. I would want to lay her down right there on the green felt and kiss her all over her body, lick the salt from the inside of her thighs. At night, when we got back home, we would take a blanket and a pillow out to the back yard. Vicky said she liked to see the stars when she got off. I'd take my saxophone out there and play it for her, too. She loved songs by George Gershwin and Johnny Mercer. Vicky especially liked "Summertime." I must have played that song for her at least fifty times.

I missed that loose, happy feeling I got from being drunk. Also I kept seeing a lot of the old crowd around. When you're used to getting drunk with someone, it just isn't the same sober. But my job at the detox house was a constant reminder of the dark side of booze, the way it can ravage a person's life. I had taken care of drunks who had been living under bridges and in abandoned cars—human scarecrows reeking of excrement and urine. I had cleaned up vomit and spoon-fed a man who was shaking so much he couldn't feed himself. Husbands brought their wives in, and wives brought their husbands in. Cops brought drunks in from jails and courthouses, and social workers brought them in. Ursa's friends in AA brought them in, too, and sometimes they would just stumble in off the street.

One night I took care of a bone-thin black woman who was distraught because the Department of Social Services had taken away her children. She kept saying she was an unfit mother and a failure as a human being. I put my arm around her and let her sob into my chest. I told her that she was a good person at heart, that she had just made a few missteps, and that like a lot of people, including me, she had a weakness for alcohol. I told her she could get her kids back—all she had to do stay off the booze and prove that she was a responsible mother. I finally managed to get her calmed down. Just when I thought she was okay, she started throwing up blood. I called 911, and by the time the rescue squad got there she had filled up one third of a wastepaper basket with blood. This really shook me up because I was afraid she was going to die.

But she made it. I called the hospital every day to check on her. She got emergency surgery, transfusions and survived.

"Drunks are tough," Ursa said, a few evenings later in the office. She usually stayed around awhile after I came onto my shift. "It's hard to kill us. We can take a lot of punishment and still survive."

Ursa had been a closet drunk. She hid bottles all over her house and indulged on the sly. "I spent years worshiping at the porcelain throne," she said. "Nobody knew it." She said her husband, a surgeon, stayed so busy with his practice he never had time for her. "Doctors," she said scornfully. "They make plenty of money, but they can be pitiful husbands and fathers." She and her husband had a daughter in college. "My husband never had time for either one of us. He lives for his work. He loves to cut into people, cut out the diseased places."

"At least he'll always have a job, with all the disease around."

"Too much sickness is in the mind. No one even knows how that works, so how can a doctor fix it when it goes wrong?"

"I don't have an answer for that," I said.

"Everybody's looking for a fix. They get drunk, shoot up, pig out, pop a pill, hoping all their prayers will be answered. I've been there. But AA saved my life. I'd be dead now if it weren't for the people in AA."

"I'm glad they were there for you."

"Who was there for you, Josh?"

"Nobody."

"You don't have to be alone. You know you can call me—anytime, any-place—if you ever feel yourself slipping."

"I appreciate that."

"Promise to call me?"

"Yes," I said. "I promise."

I usually sidestepped Ursa's questions about my personal life, but one night she wanted to know if I had a girlfriend, and I told her yes. She then launched into a tirade I had heard before, about how trashy today's young women were with their tattoos, revealing clothes, and loose morals. "American women are like stray cats—screwing everything in sight. No wonder there's so much trouble with STDs."

When Ursa got revved up like that, I suspected she was trying to get a rise out of me. So I would just listen to her with an amused smile. That only riled her more.

Ursa began staying later and later at night to talk to me. By an odd coincidence, around the same time Ursa began doing this, Vicky would get these amorous urges in the last hour before it was time for me to leave for work. Several nights a week I would rush out the door, pulling my pants on as I went, trying not to be late. I had already begun to see my job as a personal mission. Although it could be emotionally draining, I got a deep sense of satisfaction from helping those sick, scared people make it through the night. I had only been working there a couple of months when Ursa told me I had a magic touch with a person just coming off booze. She said I could calm down a wet drunk better than anyone she had ever seen.

One night Ursa stayed later than usual. We only had two residents, a woman named Mavis who lived on a farm out in the county and a wino the cops had brought in from jail. Ursa hustled them both off to bed after the evening news; then we sat there watching TV and talking. She was acting different, girlish and giggly, but I attributed her unusual behavior to the influence of the full moon.

About fifteen minutes into the late movie, she took an overnight bag into the john. When she came out she had on a red kimono, open at the front, with nothing on underneath except black, fishnet panties. She did a pirouette and asked me if I liked her outfit.

"It's okay," I said, trying to keep my eyes off her crotch. "But what about the residents?"

"They're deep in dreamland." Ursa turned the lamps off, leaving only the faint light from the pizza parlor next door, streaming through cracks in the blinds. The next thing I knew she was on my lap and her tongue was in my mouth. Even though Vicky had given me an unusually intense workout before I had left, I could feel my body responding vigorously, especially when Ursa began sitting astride my thighs, moaning and grinding herself against me. But my mind was plagued by doubt. I kept thinking about Vicky for one thing, and the fact that Ursa was married. What if her husband loved her like I had loved Iris?

Just before I felt myself losing control, I slid out from under her and stood up. "I can't go through with this."

"Why not?"

"I just can't."

"You don't find me attractive?"

"It's not that, Ursa. I just—don't like the location."

"The location makes it all the more exciting."

"Not for me."

"Well," she said, pulling her kimono shut with a flourish. "We'll just have to find a different location, then, won't we?"


"Cats," this resident was saying. "Their bottom halves were normal, but the top half was skeletons. Nothing but bones. Fucking things were all over me. I'd knock them off, but they'd get right back on."

His name was Dennis—a big, fleshy guy who managed an auto parts store. He was telling his buddy Larry about the time he had gone into DTs. AA members who had backslid on a week-long fishing trip, they were both still drunk and red as lobsters from the sun. Their wives had brought them in earlier that evening. In a couple of hours they would be sweating and probably puking, too.

I had four people to help get through the night: Dennis, Larry, Mavis, and a young man named James.

"So what do you do at work, Dennis?" I asked. I wanted to steer him away from the hallucinatory cats.

"Screw work," said Dennis.

"I know about them cats," Larry said.

"Anyone want coffee?"

"What I'd like is something stronger," Dennis said, smirking at Larry. "Wouldn't have a beer around, would you?"

"Afraid not."

"I didn't think so," Dennis said.

James, who was sitting beside Mavis on the couch, was jerking his head back and forth and blinking his eyes like he was getting hit with little electric shocks. I had tried to get him to open up a couple of times, but he answered only in monosyllables and avoided my eyes.

Dennis elbowed me in the ribs. "That nigger is making me nervous."

"He's fine," I said. "You're going to be all right, too. We're going to get you straight and back home to your wife."

"Don't know if she'll take me back."

"She'll take you back. Don't worry."

We all sat there watching TV awhile—a documentary about the Apollo astronauts' explorations of the moon.

"At first I thought that was a miracle," Mavis said. "Then I realized it wasn't a real miracle, just another example of men trying to perform one."

"Ma'am, Jack Daniels put my ass up in space plenty of times," Dennis said.

Larry said, "Jack took him all the way to the moon."

James got up and went into the bathroom. Larry began blinking his eyes and jerking his head back and forth. Dennis laughed so hard his jowls quivered.

"You all quit that foolishness," Mavis said.

"Hey, you two," I said to Dennis and Larry, "how about a game of cards?"

"Want to play for money?" Dennis asked.

"We just use poker chips around here."

I invited Mavis to play, too, but she declined.

Dennis, Larry, and I went into the kitchen and began playing poker at the table. While we played I got them talking about their fishing trip. Each one tried to outdo the other bragging about the fish he had caught.

Then Mavis came into the kitchen to tell me that James was having trouble in his room.

I found him sitting on the floor with his back against the wall, swinging his head from side to side like he was watching a ping pong game. "James," I said. "You okay, buddy?"

He didn't answer.

When I knelt beside him, he drew back as if I were a leper. "James, it's me—Josh Nichols. I'm here to help you."

He tried to speak, but he could only make guttural sounds. His eyes were wide and terrified, as if he were staring at some transcendent, evil presence in the room. I've never seen terror like that in another human being's eyes. It made the skin on my arms and back tingle.

I kept trying to calm him down, but my efforts only seemed to make him more agitated. Suddenly, he covered up his head with his arms and began crawling on his stomach to the center of the room, where he flipped over on his back and went into convulsions. I was afraid he would choke on his tongue, but he was thrashing around so wildly there was no way I could even get his mouth open.

"Oh Lord!" Mavis cried. She stood in the doorway, wearing her robe and pajamas.

"Mavis, I need you to go out into the office and call the rescue squad!"

Mavis left in a hurry, but she soon returned to tell me the phone was locked. Ursa had put a lock on the dial to prevent the residents from sneaking out there during the day and making unauthorized long distance calls. Where was the key? I had no idea. Ursa usually unlocked it before she left, but evidently she had forgotten to do it tonight.

Dennis and Larry appeared behind Mavis.

"What's wrong with him?" Dennis asked.

"Go back to the kitchen!" I told them. "This doesn't concern you."

What to do? I didn't want to leave James alone to try to get help; I was afraid he would choke on his tongue or injure himself in some way. Moreover, it was a cardinal rule for all staff members that residents were never to be left alone under any circumstances.

I kept calling his name and trying to calm him down, but he was beyond my reach. The only thing I could think of to do was pray, something I hadn't done much of in recent years. It took me awhile to get going good. I was bereft in the prayer department.

I was still praying when Mavis returned to tell me the rescue squad was on the way. She had called them from the pizza parlor next door.

When I got home from my shift, Vicky was already up, cooking pancakes.

"Rough night?" she asked.

I told her about James. Before the rescue squad had taken him to the hospital, one of the attendants had assured me he would live. I wanted to tell Vicky about the terror I had seen in James's eyes and how frustrated and unnerved I had felt trying to reach him. And I wanted to tell her about how I had finally gotten the residents down to sleep and was trying to relax on the couch when I pictured the astronauts—walking on the moon in their space suits, breathing oxygen from tanks on their backs—and, as I imagined myself in that alien, barren place, my heart felt like it had been snake-bit. What if something had gone wrong up there and their spacecraft wouldn't fire up? No one would have been able to save them. Just thinking about it again made my throat tighten up. But when I tried to talk about this to Vicky, I felt lightheaded, like I was standing on the edge of an abyss.

I thanked her for breakfast and went back to the bedroom to lie down. She had already hung the black plastic over the blinds. Soon she came in and lay beside me. At first my breath was fast and irregular, but after awhile I was breathing in time with her. Deep and slow. I felt comforted by her presence, her scent of pancakes and maple syrup.

*You're a good man, Josh.* I'm sure Vicky whispered those words just before I drifted off to sleep. I know it's not something I dreamed.

# Shipwrecks

When I was five years old my twin brother, Caleb, killed my pet rabbit. Our mother had given each of us a white rabbit for Easter, but after his died mysteriously, he wanted to play with mine. I pushed him away. "My bunny." Later, I found my rabbit lying by the piano bench, a drop of blood on its mouth, its ruby eyes suspended between sleep and wakefulness. I showed my mother the corpse, expecting her to administer swift, apocalyptic punishment, but instead she took Caleb into her bedroom and talked to him in a plaintive voice. *Why did you kill Brett's rabbit?* Through the partially opened door I watched her hold him in her lap, stroking his hair as if he were the injured party rather than I.

Caleb, my fraternal twin, was sickly as a small child. He endured several operations on his inner ear, which always seemed to be draining. Pale and thin, with heavy-lidded eyes, he had a fiercely independent streak that belied his frail appearance. When Lavinia, who took care of us while our mother worked, prayed before meals, he rarely closed his eyes. And once, after she told him Jesus was the only perfect person who had ever lived, he said, "I don't see why he was so perfect. All he did was get himself killed to prove a point. What's the big deal about that?"

"The Devil's got your tongue, child," said Lavinia. And in her later account of Caleb's comment to our mother, Lavinia tried to convince her to take us to church. "Them boys is almost eight years old. Time for them to be hearing the word of God."

My mother was disdainful of our housekeeper's faith. "All those holy rollers leave me cold," she told me later. "I don't like the idea of Lavinia speaking in tongues around you boys, either. That's just a bunch of gibberish."

It was true that Lavinia occasionally became so overcome during prayer that she would speak in tongues, which made my brother roll his eyes.

Unlike Caleb, I regarded Lavinia's indecipherable stream of syllables as holy incantations. I listened to her sermons with reverence, paying keen attention to the stories of how Jesus had healed the sick, raised the dead, and driven demons from the souls of the possessed. I learned, however, not to discuss these miraculous events with my mother, for she dismissed our housekeeper's accounts of Jesus as fairy tales. She added, "Only literal-minded people believe them."

My mother, who had us at thirty-nine, worked six days a week as a reporter on the morning edition of the city's newspaper. She went to work in the early afternoon and didn't come home until after midnight. Lavinia would fall asleep on the sofa, and my mother would drive her home, leaving us unattended until she got back. One night I woke up from a nightmare, and when I cried out for Lavinia, neither she nor my mother answered.

My cry awakened my brother, whose bed was beside mine. He asked me what was wrong, and I told him we were all alone. "So what?" he said. "Go back to sleep."

But I couldn't sleep. My heart pounded as I listened to the wind moaning in the eaves. Three weeks earlier hunters had discovered a woman in the woods, less than a mile from our house, stabbed to death. What if her killer were still around? I imagined he was outside, rattling the windows, trying to get in. What if he killed our mother? As I shivered with terror I could hear my brother snoring. How I envied his indifference to the possibility of danger.

I stayed awake until I heard my mother's car engine outside, her keys jingling, her footsteps moving over the floor, and smelled the faint fragrance of her Evening in Paris perfume.

Only then could I sleep.

We lived in a valley surrounded by mountains. Coal miners descended shafts deep beneath the rock, where they occasionally died in mine cave-ins. On Saturdays I saw them in town—stern, quiet men, their faces stained by the black coal dust.

All we knew about our father was his name, Karl Adams. "When he found out I was pregnant with twins he decided to take a long ocean voyage," Mother told us. We had no idea what he looked like. My mother, Florence Adams, never tried to find him or contact him to tell him how we were doing. This was a mystery to me.

One winter Lavinia shattered her hip in a fall, and afterwards she was unable to care for us. My mother hired different sitters, but after we lost Lavinia it was as if we were jinxed. No one ever stayed more than a few months. Oftentimes my brother and I would come home from school and be greeted by a stranger. "I'm Mrs. Davis," our new sitter would say, or "I'm Jean. Which one of you is Brett and which one is Caleb?"

My brother and I were constantly fighting. Caleb argued with our mother, too, calling her hateful names. Once he even threatened to kill her. When he began failing in school, my mother took us both to see a psychiatrist named Dr. Vernon, who I never saw smile. Although neither my brother nor I liked him, my mother seemed smitten with Dr. Vernon, and after our meetings with him, she would send us out and talk with him behind a closed door. A few months after our sessions with the psychiatrist began, my mother asked my brother if he would like to stay for a while with her sister, Harriet, and her husband Ralph, on their chicken farm in upstate New York. To my surprise, Caleb agreed. Although I was not close to my brother I was used to his presence in my life, and I was troubled by the idea of his leaving. I asked my mother why he had to go live with our aunt and uncle.

"Dr. Vernon thinks you boys should be separated," she said. "And Aunt Harriet has never liked you."

It was true; my aunt and I didn't get along. Once, after I tried to play a song on the piano for her, she accused me of being a showoff who always had to be the center of attention.

Before she sent my brother to live with her sister, my mother got out her Ouija board and asked me to help her summon her spirit guides. We consulted the Ouija board whenever my mother needed advice or had to make a difficult decision. She would present a silent question to the spirits, and I would sit with my hand on the board until it began moving. Since my brother refused to cooperate with her efforts to contact her spirit guides, she always asked me to help. During these times I felt as if I had my mother all to myself.

When she consulted her Ouija board Mother closed her eyes, asking her questions in silence. I would stare at our two hands on the plastic guide and wait for it to move. It would move slowly at first, then more authoritatively, sometimes to either Yes or No; other times, it would move in a circular motion, lingering at various letters before moving on. My mother would stare at the letters as if transfixed, her eyes alarmingly fierce, like a cat staring at a bird. If she were dissatisfied with a reading she would scowl and say the spirits weren't getting through, and we would put the board up until later. But this time she seemed satisfied. She returned the Ouija board to its box, and I put it behind the couch.

A few days later she drove us to the bus station so Caleb could make the eleven-hour trip to my aunt and uncle's farm in New York. I sat beside my brother, our legs and arms touching.

"Are you afraid?" I asked, when my mother went in to the station to buy his ticket.

"Of what—a bunch of chickens?"

Before Caleb got on the bus my mother held him tightly, tears streaming from her eyes, which were a beautiful shade of violet. "Goodbye, darling," she said. "Remember Mother loves you. I'll write you soon."

She cried all the way home.

Caleb visited us at Christmas and for a few weeks in the summer, but he expressed little interest in moving back home. He declared he liked living with our aunt and uncle. He was not only making decent grades in school but had also learned to drive a tractor and shoot a rifle. "Only problem is Aunt Harriet stays on my ass about chores and homework," he said.

My mother took a week off from work and drove us up to see him. My aunt and uncle lived in a dingy farmhouse with several long, wooden buildings out back. One of the buildings contained vats of water full of thousands of dead chicks. My uncle Ralph explained that he only raised hens for their eggs and that he drowned the male chicks and sold their bodies for fertilizer.

"That seems like a waste," I said.

"You have a problem with it, you can always give up eating eggs," my uncle said. "That way you'll have a clean conscience."

When Caleb and I were alone he challenged me to a race, which he easily won. He was taller than I was and his body sinewy with muscle. His voice was changing, too.

I asked when he was coming home.

"Nothing back there but hillbillies."

"That's where you're from."

"It's where you're going that matters."

"Where are you going?"

"Far away from the Adams sisters. You don't get it, do you?"

"Get what?"

"You know all those chicks Uncle Ralph drowns? Sometimes when he looks at them he pictures her there instead."

"Aunt Harriet?"

Caleb nodded and spat on the ground. "Know how you run, Brett? Flat-footed. Like a man with a bag of rocks on his back."

The year I turned fourteen my mother and I moved to New Jersey, where she had gotten a job working on a larger newspaper that paid her a higher salary. In this new city smoke from factories darkened the sky and tainted the air with an acrid smell. My mother rented a three-room apartment and enrolled me in a nearby school, where the other students mocked my mountain accent. Once, in a fight after school, a bigger, older boy beat me up so badly that both my eyes swelled shut. Other than Sundays my mother was rarely home. Afternoons and evenings I hung out at a delicatessen, gambling with some Puerto Rican boys by pitching coins against the sides of buildings. I ate supper alone in our apartment. My bed was in an alcove just off the kitchen. A fire escape led from the kitchen window down to an alley below. At night I lay in bed listening to the sounds of the city—cars honking, cats yowling, voices echoing in the alley. I dreamed of a tall, gray-haired man, more handsome than either Caleb or I, standing at the bow of a ship, breathing clean sea air.

One afternoon when I got home from school I was shocked to see Caleb sitting in the window by the fire escape. His eyes were bloodshot, with dark half moons underneath.

"Caleb! What are you doing here?"

"Aunt Harriet was planning to send me up the river."

"What are you talking about?"

"I'm talking about bars, fool. Locked up with a bunch of butt-fuckers."

"Why would she do that?"

Caleb said his relationship with Aunt Harriet had steadily deteriorated during the past year, especially after he had started messing up at school. She had begun taking away his privileges, grounding him and banishing him to his room. Finally, she had given him an ultimatum—either stop sassing her and improve his grades or she was going to have him committed to a state home for boys. Two days later his suspension from school for truancy had triggered a fierce argument between them. Caleb said Aunt Harriet told him she was calling the police to take him to reform school. She said she had already signed the necessary papers, adding, "All they have to do is pick you up." My brother went upstairs to his room, climbed out the window, shimmied down the drainpipe, ran into the woods, and hitchhiked south. He had located our apartment from an address on a letter Aunt Harriet had written our mother, informing her that she might have him committed for being incorrigible.

"Why didn't you just get the address off the letters Mother sent every week with the checks?"

"Checks? I never heard about any checks. Harriet told me she and Uncle Ralph paid for everything. That's part of why I worked so hard for them. Figured I was earning my keep."

"But Mother sent money for you every week."

"She did, huh. Harriet is even more of a lying bitch than I thought."

I was not happy to have Caleb living with us again. He was much stronger than I, and he began bullying me. When we were younger I had been able to overpower him easily, but now when I tried to fight him he would knock me to the floor with a flurry of lightning-quick blows. Although my mother had enrolled him in school she had little control over him. He refused to obey simple requests like clearing the table or picking up his dirty socks from the floor. After he got suspended from school for fighting she consulted the Ouija board. Believing I knew her question I carefully directed the guide to *send him back to harriet*. But when my mother called her sister to discuss Caleb, they began arguing, and my mother ended up hanging up on her.

"Harriet couldn't have children of her own, and I thought having Caleb would be good for her and Ralph," she said. "Some mother she'd have been. Her children would have ended up in state institutions! Not only that, she lied to Caleb about the money I sent. I don't know how Ralph stands her."

"He spends a lot of time out in the chicken houses," Caleb said. My mother laughed, and she and my brother exchanged a knowing look.

With Caleb back in our lives my mother became much more remote with me. While my brother was gone she had enjoyed listening to me play the piano, a battered Wurlitzer we had moved with us to New Jersey, and if she were not too tired from her job she would take an interest in my life, asking me questions about school, encouraging me to do my homework and to make good grades. But all of that ended with Caleb's return; now she was completely focused on him. She stocked the kitchen and refrigerator with his favorite foods. If he and I fought she invariably took his side. If I showed her an exam with an A on it, her mind was somewhere else. ("That's nice, Brett, now let me read the paper.") But if Caleb showed her one of his sketches she lavished praise on him for his artistic talent. Caleb, who often stayed home from school, spent most of his time playing with his white mice, which he kept in cages by his bed, reading comic books, or drawing

174

pictures for my mother to admire—hornets swarming out of a hive or a skeleton lashing a bird from the air with a bullwhip.

I looked forward to the times my mother consulted the Ouija board, when I could feel the familiar current connecting our hands as they moved in unison on the guide, lingering over the letters that answered her silent questions to the spirits.

Caleb's return home seemed to usher in a time of bad luck for us. My mother changed jobs four times in three years, and we moved often. She was fired from one job, laid off from another, and a company she worked for went out of business. Although I attended schools everywhere we lived, I failed some classes and ended up repeating the ninth grade. My brother stopped going to school altogether, which led to numerous arguments between him and my mother. Once, during a particularly ugly fight, my mother threatened to have him put in jail. Later that evening I found Caleb unconscious on the floor, an empty bottle of my mother's sleeping pills beside him. At the hospital doctors pumped his stomach while my mother sat in a chair in the lobby, her face pale and stricken. I paced the floor, terrified Caleb was going to die. I prayed—something I hadn't done in years—begging God to let my brother live. I made promises that I never kept. My brother survived, and afterwards Mother never mentioned school again.

Caleb began working at gas stations, eventually learning how to repair cars. At seventeen, he bought a black Corvette he claimed would go 130 miles per hour. After he came home from work he would lie on the living room sofa in greasy mechanic's coveralls. Because of the stained sofa and the dilapidated house we were renting, I was ashamed to invite my friends home. The front porch had rotting boards, and the roof leaked when it rained.

We were living in Alabama, where my mother was a reporter and Caleb a mechanic in an auto repair shop. We had moved to that town in the middle of my sophomore year. That year I made nearly all A's on my report cards. My junior year I was placed in accelerated classes and elected to the student council. I wore white shirts and neatly pressed trousers. I wrote poetry and articles for the school newspaper and played the piano in talent shows. My positive new attitude in school was motivated, in part, by a desire to earn my mother's approval. In addition to my success at school I kept the house clean—the floor mopped and the dishes washed. My brother, a high school dropout in grease-stained coveralls, left ashtrays full of cigarette butts around the house for me to empty, packs of rubbers on the kitchen counter with his keys and change, and he flew hot if my mother tried to make him do anything he didn't want to do. My mother still doted on him.

I wondered if I had some hidden defect that made me less worthy of love.

At school one day I passed by the incinerators where the boys in vocational classes smoked cigarettes. A group of them had picked up Odell Duncan, a retarded boy, and they were pushing him head first into a trash can. I shoved them aside. As I was helping Odell out of the trash can, a tall, weasel-faced kid named Rex Gilroy punched me in the face. He was fast and he hit hard, but I got in a few good punches before two of his friends jumped me and pinned me to the ground. "I'm going to stomp your face into jelly," Rex said.

Before Rex could make good on his threat, I heard an authoritative voice ring out: "Gilroy, you boys turn him loose and clear out of here if you don't want to be suspended. And I mean right now!"

It was Mr. Gordon, my geometry teacher. "Adams, you stay here, I want to talk to you."

After the others left, Mr. Gordon said he had seen the boys putting Odell into the trash can from a window on the second floor, and while he admired me for interceding, he pointed out that I had too much to lose by fighting roughnecks like Rex Gilroy. "I'm going to keep an eye on them," he said. "In the meantime, you need to stay away from Rex and his friends. If they say anything to you, don't answer. Just keep walking."

That afternoon a boy stopped me in the hall and told me Rex was going to kill me.

"I don't think so," I said, with false bravado.

"Come to the game tonight, and you'll find out. He told me to tell you he'll be waiting for you."

Being the new kid at so many schools had taught me that timidity only encouraged bullies like Rex. I knew I had to go to the game. I asked a few of my friends at school to go with me, but they didn't want to get involved. They advised me to stay home.

I had no choice but to ask my brother for help. After he came home from work I sat beside him on the living room sofa awhile before I told him what had happened. He was in his soiled coveralls, watching TV.

"Who'd you fight?" He seemed more amused than curious.

"Rex Gilroy and his buddies. They're going to jump me tonight at the football game."

"Punks."

"Can you go with me?" I held my breath while my brother stared at the TV, smoke from his cigarette curling up around his face.

"What times does the game start?"

"Seven o'clock."

"Be ready at a quarter till. I got to be somewhere at seven-thirty."

That night when I rode up to the high school football field in my brother's Corvette, I saw Rex waiting with a crowd of his friends at the gate.

Caleb parked by the curb, revving up the engine a couple of times before we got out and walked towards the gate. I suddenly felt guilty for involving him in my fight. Now we would both be hurt, maybe even killed. Why hadn't I taken my friends' advice and stayed home?

But when we approached Rex, his eyes were fixed meekly on my brother.

"Hey, Caleb," he said.

"I hear we got some unfinished business," my brother said.

"Not with me."

"You said you were going to kill me," I pointed out.

"Nah, man. I was just mad. I didn't mean it. Let's just forget the whole thing."

"How about them?" Caleb pointed at Rex's friends. They looked quickly away.

"They don't want any trouble, either." To demonstrate his sincerity Rex offered me his hand.

On the way back to my brother's car I touched his arm. "Thanks, Caleb. I really appreciate your help."

"You ought to stay away from punks like that. They might screw up your image."

I was deeply impressed by the way my brother had cowed Rex Gilroy and his friends. It made me see he had a whole life I knew nothing about.

Unlike most of my friends, I had no girlfriend. Part of the problem was my lack of access to a car. My mother rarely let me drive her Plymouth. A girl in my English class had shown an interest in me, and I finally got up enough nerve to invite her to the junior-senior prom. I was thrilled when she accepted.

I asked my mother if I could use her car for the prom.

"Caleb needs my car," she said. His Corvette, which had blown a head gasket, was under a tarp in the driveway. "Why can't you ask the girl to pick you up?"

"It's the prom, the social event of the year. I have to drive."

"Ask Caleb. If he says it's okay you can use it for the night."

"Why should I have to ask him? It's your car."

"Ask him, Brett."

Although it angered me to do it I asked my brother if I could use the car for the prom.

"I'm using the car that night," he said.

"You drive that damn car all the time, and I only need it for one night. Why can't you let me use it?"

"Can't do it, schoolboy."

All of the anger I had been holding in against my mother and brother crystallized over the issue of the car, and I was determined to have access to it. A week before the prom I asked my mother again if I could borrow her car. When she told me to ask Caleb, I lost my temper. I accused her of loving him more than me and told her I hated them both.

Caleb came into the living room. "Why don't you get one of your hot-shot friends to drive you?"

"Goddamn you!" I shouted. "Goddamn you both to hell!"

Caleb held up the car keys, jingling them in front of his face. Smiling, he walked backwards into the kitchen. I followed him to the door and cursed him as he went outside, got into my mother's Plymouth, revved up the engine, and drove away.

My mother came into the kitchen.

"Mother—"

"I want you to hush, Brett."

Caleb had left a glass jar for one of his pet mice on the kitchen counter. In a rage I picked it up and slammed it against the counter. Slivers of glass were imbedded in my skin. My right ring finger looked nearly cut in half.

"Good God!" my mother said.

I pressed my bloody hands against my shirt. My mother got out a broom and a dustpan and began sweeping up the glass.

"I need to see a doctor," I said, feeling faint.

"I want to sweep up this glass first. I don't want Caleb to step on it when he comes back."

At the ER a doctor cleaned my wounds, sewing up the ones that needed stitches. I had severed a tendon in my right ring finger. "I can't fix that," he said. "You'll have to see a specialist."

I stayed home the night of the prom. I could no longer move my right ring finger. I wondered if I would ever be able to play the piano again.

My mother drove me to Montgomery to see a surgeon, a hand specialist, who said I would need a tendon transplant. Using a section of tendon from my wrist he would reconstruct the tendon in my right ring finger. During the five-hour operation he would graft the new tendon to the knuckles on my ring finger and run it down through my palm to my wrist. "Because tendons stretch we have to make them shorter," he said. "Otherwise they'd lack enough tension to work again." Afterwards, I would need to follow a prescribed regimen of therapy, wearing splints at night and doing exercises to stretch the tendon. Although I should be able to play the piano, I would never regain complete range of motion in that finger.

I woke up from the surgery with my right arm in a cast, suspended from a device above the bed. My hand felt as if someone were pounding nails through the palm and ring finger. Every four hours a nurse gave me a shot of morphine to ease the pain.

When my mother and brother came to take me back home, Mother showered attention on me—fixing the back seat up with a pillow and a thermos of ice water for the hundred-mile drive home. While Caleb drove I dozed, still groggy from the anesthesia. I woke up from a half-sleep, craving chocolate milk. I told my mother what I wanted, and she asked my brother to pull off the two-lane road. He stopped in front of a country store next to a newly plowed field.

"Can you get his milk?"

"Don't feel like it," he said.

"I'll get it, then," she said. Why was she always deferring to him?

"I want Caleb to get it!"

"Screw off." I saw the reflection of Caleb's eyes, hooded and sullen, in the rearview mirror.

With my left hand I opened the rear door of the sedan. I got out and slammed the door shut. My brother backed onto the road and the car shot forward, leaving a strip of rubber on the pavement. I watched the car speed down the road, vanishing around a bend in the distance. Why didn't my mother make him come back? Why didn't she have any control over him? I was barefoot, wearing blue jeans, a white cotton shirt thrown over my shoulders. In the hot noon sun I walked out onto the field, stepping over chunks of red earth. I couldn't stop crying. My right hand throbbed and ached with every beat of my heart. I sat on the ground and watched a buzzard trace a lazy circle against the clouds.

As if in a dream I saw my mother's Plymouth pull up to the edge of the field. Stumbling toward the car I picked up a stone with my left hand and hid it under my shirt. If my brother attacked me I planned to smash it against his skull.

But Caleb wasn't in the car. My mother was driving. I got into the back seat, and she turned the car around and headed back to the road that ran north.

"Where's Caleb?" The stone was cold against my heart.

"I kept telling him to stop, and he finally pulled off the road and jumped out. I don't know why you two can't get along any better than you do."

"He drives off and leaves me barefoot beside the road with my arm in a cast, and you're not even mad at him?"

My mother didn't answer.

After we had gone a few miles I saw Caleb leaning against a pine beside the road. My mother stopped on the roadside and waited while he walked to the car. She slid over and let him take the wheel.

We rode the rest of the way home in silence.

In our driveway, when I got out of the car, my brother watched me toss the stone into the grass.

"What did you plan to do with that?"

"You never gave me a chance to find out."

"Tough talk from a one-armed boy."

I went into the house, up the stairs to my room.

You're dead, Caleb, I thought. From this moment on you no longer exist.

My mother was late to my high school graduation. She was arranging bail for Caleb, who had been jailed on a DUI charge. She entered the gym as I was descending the stage. When she hugged me she reeked of Caleb's cigarettes. She looked sad and troubled, her mind still on my brother.

I went to the University of Alabama in Tuscaloosa on a modest academic scholarship. My mother helped out when she could, but I mostly worked my way through, managing to graduate cum laude with a double major in business and computer programming. Caleb had moved back to our hometown in the mountains, where he was working as the night manager of a twenty-four-hour Texaco. Soon after he returned to our hometown my mother went back there, too. She got her old job back at the newspaper.

Although I saw her infrequently, I stayed in touch with my mother by telephone and letter. She kept me informed of their lives, including her efforts to help Caleb out of various jams. By the time he was thirty he had been married three times, fathered two children, and been jailed several times for assault and battery. He had owned thirty-seven vehicles and totaled five of them in wrecks. Once my mother called to report he was deeply upset because he had shot his dog in the living room of his house after it bared its teeth at him. He drove around for three days with the dog in the trunk of his car before my mother took it out and buried it. "He loved that dog," she said. "He was so devastated he couldn't eat."

My mother continued working after she reached retirement age. She used her Social Security income to help my brother buy a four-acre lot in the country and begin building a house. "Caleb has always wanted a place of his own," my mother wrote. "He feels inadequate because he's had to rent." He was married again with a baby on the way.

When my brother began building his house I had just been promoted to marketing director for the southeastern district of a Charlotte-based Internet services company. My wife, Leah, whom I had met at the University of Alabama, was an allergist. Our twins, Gabriel and Nerissa, were a year old. Leah and I were earning more money than we needed, so on Christmas I sent my brother a check for five thousand dollars to help with the house. Although he never thanked me for the money, he sent me a Christmas card, enclosing photos of the house-in-progress and his new baby, a daughter.

Caleb and his wife separated before he could complete the house. "Yvonne never made him feel loved," my mother wrote. Their unfinished house sat empty for a year before my brother and his wife sold it for twenty percent of what my mother had spent on it. Yvonne used her share of the money to buy a car for her boyfriend, according to my mother. Caleb paid for some dental work for his new girlfriend, a waitress he had met in a bowling alley. He also made a couple of late child support payments and bought a motorcycle.

"I gave him more than two years of my salary," my mother said bitterly. "And look what he's got to show for it."

"You need to let Caleb make his own way in the world. He's a grown man now."

My mother seemed not to have heard me.

"I don't know how he'll ever get a house now, with all of the child support payments he has to make."

Caught up in the demands of my job and my wife and children, I didn't see my mother or brother for nearly four years. One Saturday morning he called to tell me that he and his new wife were in Charlotte, on their way back home from their honeymoon at the beach. He asked if he could stop by. I said sure, and I invited him to spend the night.

Caleb drove up to our five-bedroom brick colonial in a rusted Dodge pickup with a shot muffler. I saw him from my window, and I walked down the driveway to greet him and his new wife, a rail-thin platinum blonde with lavender eye shadow. Caleb's jeans hung low on his narrow hips. He had a jagged scar on his cheek.

"Howdy, Brett," he said, offering me his callused hand. "This is Georgette."

"Hello, Georgette. Nice to meet you."

My brother's wife looked me boldly up and down, like I was a horse she was thinking about buying. "I can't believe you two are actually twins."

"Fraternal, not identical."

"He got all the luck," Caleb said.

"What did you get?"

"I just got you."

Georgette's laugh reminded me of someone choking on a piece of meat.

I said, "Come on in and meet my family."

Gabriel and Nerissa, who had just turned five, were thrilled to meet their uncle Caleb. My brother held them, one on each knee, and posed for photographs. That afternoon he and Georgette went to K-Mart and returned with their arms full of gifts for our children. When Leah protested Caleb said, "This is to make up for the Christmases you didn't hear from me."

My wife let Georgette help with supper. Leah, the only child of an internist, had grown up in a house with a full-time maid, and although her work as a physician had enlarged her experience with people, my brother's wife kept her somewhat off balance. On my way into the kitchen to get Caleb a drink, I overheard Georgette say, "Girl, a big one just feels better." Leah's face was a polite mask.

After I put my children to bed my brother and I sat out on the patio, drinking whiskey and trying to connect with each other. Caleb told me he was taking flying lessons and hoped to buy his own airplane. He and Georgette had just put a down payment on a mobile home. He said he was looking for a lot in the country but until he could find one, he had set it up in a trailer park. I resisted my urge to tell him that my salespeople had surpassed their monthly goals for three straight months or mention our stock portfolio. But as sat I across from my brother on my stone patio, my stomach full of shrimp Creole and fine Kentucky bourbon, I felt surrounded by love and good luck. And, after my third glass of whiskey, I couldn't help but mention our one-third interest in an oceanfront motel. A year earlier Leah and I had invested in the Nags Head motel, along with two of her colleagues and their spouses. We had a manager, a retired Navy man named Albert. For Leah and her colleagues the motel was a tax write-off and a way to build equity. Plus we had a free place to stay at the beach.

"You're doing all right for yourself, Brett," Caleb said, flipping a cigarette onto the lawn. "You're lucky to watch your kids grow up, too. I hardly ever get to see mine."

"Sorry to hear that," I said. But I thought, whose fault is that?

The next morning as he was leaving my brother backed his truck into my new Volvo, smashing the headlight and crumpling the right fender. He said his insurance premiums were already more than he could afford due to his numerous accidents, so I told him I would take care of it. It was a small price to pay for the satisfaction I got from being able to dangle my good fortune before my brother's eyes—the same way he had dangled the keys to my mother's car in front of mine so many years before.

My mother began calling me to complain she was losing her memory. She couldn't remember her phone number or the name of the nursing home her sister, Harriet, was staying in. I called my brother and talked to him awhile about his personal life before I got around to asking him about Mother. He assured me she was all right, that he checked on her two or three times a week. "She's just old, that's all. Same thing is gonna happen to all of us if we live long enough."

But a few months later my brother called to say that our mother had been wandering around her neighborhood in her nightgown. "I got a woman to stay with her during the day, but Mother ran her off. Nobody can do anything with her."

The next time Caleb called he said Mother had been leaving the gas on in the oven. "Georgette and me don't have room for her at our place. And, anyway, she'd drive us crazy if we had to live with her."

We agreed it was time to put her in a nursing home.

My wife and children went with me to see her. Mother was fastened to the chair by a harness, to keep her safe, according to the attendant. My brother had told me she would wander the halls, bother the other residents, and try to leave the building if she weren't kept in restraints. At seventy-five, she had a dowager's hump and sparse, silver hair. Her once lovely violet eyes were milky with cataracts. There were photographs of my brother's three children on shelves in her room, two photos of Caleb, and a small portrait of Leah and me with our twins. On the television in front of her chair a young woman was skating on ice, but there was no sound.

My mother, who called me Caleb, couldn't maintain a thought long enough to engage in a conversation. She stared blankly at her grandchildren when they spoke to her. She had visited us soon after they were born, when her mind was still fairly sharp, but she hadn't seen them since. Growing restless, Gabriel and Nerissa began imitating the figure skater on TV, pretending to ice skate on the carpet. Their activity disturbed my mother. She strained at her harness, babbling and pointing.

"What is it, Mrs. Adams?" Leah asked, after she had calmed the children down. "How can we help?"

But my mother was beyond help. "Is he coming? Is he coming?" She kept asking that question.

"Is who coming, Mother?"

My mother struggled a long time to articulate the name of whomever she was waiting for before she finally gave up. Tears slid down her cheeks.

"We have to go now." I kissed her forehead. "I'll come back again soon. I promise."

She clutched my hand. "Don't leave. Please don't leave me."

Her anguished voice followed us down the long hall.

I am still haunted by that image of my mother, frail and broken, begging me not to leave her alone. She had spent most of her life working for newspapers, and what did she have to show for it? Her stories were long forgotten, and her world had shrunk to a small room where she was tied to a chair, fed and bathed by strangers—waiting for someone whose name she couldn't remember.

I had never discussed my mother with Leah in much depth, but driving back to North Carolina, I told her how my mother had never believed in anything other than her spirit guides and her newspaper work. I told her of my mother's twisted love for Caleb and how beautiful she was to me when I was a boy—how I would try to stay awake at night, just so I could see her when she came home. And I told her how she had always said she was going to retire some day and buy a cabin overlooking a lake. "She said she didn't need a man, she would have a cat for company, and she would spend her days painting with water colors and writing her memoir. She said Caleb and I would visit her, too, with our wives and children. She would bake us muffins and take our children for walks in the woods, where she would teach them the names of trees and flowers. And she would tell them entertaining stories about her boys growing up."

"I don't see how Grandma Adams stands it in that place, the horrible way it smells," Gabriel said, from the back seat. "What does she do all day besides look at that dumb television?"

Leah touched my shoulder. "Let me know if you want me to drive, Brett."

"Bad luck and heartache usually come in threes," Lavinia told me once. Her comment turned out to be prophetic for me in the ninth year of my marriage. That year my company cut a third of its work force in a major downsizing, and overnight I went from being a marketing director with a six-figure income to an unemployed househusband, my days occupied by child care, cooking, cleaning, and yard maintenance. The economic downturn had hit the communications sector especially hard, and my efforts to find another job produced no credible prospects. In an attempt to keep my spirits up I joined a support group, but I stopped going after a few sessions. What the hell, I told myself, it was just a job, and my wife makes enough to support us until I can find another one.

I soon learned that I couldn't count on Leah. Not long after I lost my job she turned cold in bed. I attributed the problem to my loss of income, which drove me into a deep depression. But that wasn't the issue. The underlying source of our estrangement was the second appearance of misfortune: a handsome dermatologist in her office complex named Tony Devereaux, with whom my wife had been playing tennis. After several late-night discussions about the problems in our marriage, Leah tearfully confessed that she and Tony were having an affair. "It just happened, Brett. I tried to resist it for months, but the attraction was too powerful."

"Jesus, Leah," I said. I was having trouble getting my breath. "How could you do this to me? How could you do this to our children?"

Leah said she'd try to stop seeing him, but that wasn't good enough for me: I told her I was moving out. She argued against this step, but not quite fervently enough to convince me to stay. I assumed she was still seeing her lover, and she made no attempt to convince me otherwise. Not wanting to stay in Charlotte, I called Albert and told him I would be needing a motel room for a while. He promised to save me an oceanfront room and to give me some suggestions on surfcasting.

Leah told our children, "Daddy is going down to the beach to look after our investment there. We're not sure how long he'll be gone." Both Gabriel and Nerissa begged to go with me, which sent Leah out of the room in tears. The day I left, Gabriel hid in my trunk, but Nerissa told Leah where he was, and she called me on the car phone to tell me I had a stowaway.

I could hear the surf in my motel room, but I had trouble sleeping at night. I missed Gabriel and Nerissa, and I couldn't stop worrying about them. What if they began failing in school? Would Gabriel start wetting his bed again? Our brief conversations on the phone were awkward and painful. I missed Leah, too: her scent, her face, the sound of her voice. I was tortured by images of her and Tony Devereaux in all the positions of love. I pictured myself doing various things to Tony—like showing up at his office with a pistol and shooting him dead in front of Leah and his office staff. When my thoughts became too powerful I would escape by getting blind drunk. I kept telling myself I needed a plan for my life, but my will was paralyzed; I felt as if I were falling through black, empty space. An insidious voice kept whispering that I was a miserable failure who couldn't even motivate his salespeople to meet their marketing goals, let alone keep his wife satisfied.

I was hanging on to the tenuous possibility that Leah would get Tony Devereaux out of her system and beg me to come home, declaring she had really loved me all along. I was immersed in a fantasy about this event one morning when the phone rang. I picked it up, thinking it was Leah, but it was Caleb—calling to tell me that Mother had died of pneumonia.

"She died around three A.M. I waited till morning to call you. Didn't want to wake you up."

"Jesus Christ."

"When the ambulance got her to the hospital, doctor said he didn't think she'd make it. Her face was blue."

"Was she alone?"

"No. I stayed there with her. Held her hand and talked to her the whole—" Caleb's voice broke. "I watched her take her last breath."

I thanked him for calling and got off the phone. I didn't know what to say to him. And I don't think he had anything else to say to me. We weren't close enough to share each other's grief, to hear each other cry.

I was waiting for Caleb at the airport below the Wright Memorial in Kill Devil Hills when he flew down from the mountains in a borrowed Cessna. He seemed proud of the plane, although it wasn't much to look at. It sat slightly cockeyed, as of one tire were smaller than the other. Rips in the faded seats had been covered up with electrician's tape. Caleb said he had gotten his pilot's license a few months earlier, not long after he and Georgette had split up. I had wondered why she hadn't been with him at my mother's funeral—Caleb had just said she was out of town. Thinking my brother had had enough trouble for one lifetime, I asked if there was any hope for reconciliation.

"About as much chance for you to change into a Chinaman."

"I'm sorry to hear that."

"That's the way it goes."

"You doing okay?"

"Yeah. Let's get this over with."

The metal urn containing my mother's ashes was on the floor on the passenger's side of the Cessna. Caleb had brought it down to the Outer Banks so we could spread her ashes at sea, in accordance with my mother's will. I sat in the passenger's seat, holding the urn in my lap. Caleb turned the key in the ignition. When the engine started, a cloud of black smoke blew out from under the hood.

"Is this thing safe to fly?"

"Got me down here, didn't it?"

My brother taxied down the runway, the engine backfiring once, and then we were airborne, rising up over the trees and out to sea, the dull silver nose of the plane glinting in the sun. Caleb flew south toward Hatteras. Off to my right I could see the brown marsh, the sound streaked white with wind-churned foam. Below us the sea shimmered like a silver sheet of ice. Our shifting position relative to the water created slow changes in the intensity of illumination. This changing surface of the sea, along with the hypnotic motion of the waves, made me feel as if I were dreaming. I thought I could see the shadowy hulls of sunken ships, still holding the bones of drowned sailors.

"Albert, the motel manager, told me you can see shipwrecks from the air," I said. "There's a lot of them at Diamond Shoals, near the lighthouse. Some of them have been there for centuries."

"You're a real hot shot, ain't you? Got your own motel and a manager, too."

Caleb didn't know about my reversals of fortune. My wife and children had flown to my hometown for my mother's funeral. While a minister my mother had never met eulogized her life on earth, Caleb, Leah, the twins, and I sat on the front pew of the church—the perfect image of a grieving family. After the service I drove back to the Outer Banks, alone. As I looked at my brother's taut face I realized that he would still see me as the one with all the luck, who had left him behind in a cloud of dust. A man generously compensated for his skills in marketing and technology. A man with a loving family and a big brick home on the rich side of town. But that picture was just an illusion now. I was unemployed, with a rapidly diminishing bank account, I lived alone in a motel room, I didn't know when I would see my children again, and my wife was sleeping with another man. Stuck by the irony of this, I began to laugh.

Caleb gave me a quizzical glance.

"All set?" I asked.

"Let me slow her down first."

The sun came out from behind a cloud, lighting up the particles of dust whirling in the cockpit. I took the top off the urn and pulled out the plastic bag containing my mother's ashes. I slid back the window, and when Caleb gave me the nod I began dumping her ashes outside.

But the wind blew them back into the plane.

"Throw the whole thing out," my brother shouted, above the rushing wind. "Just throw it out, you dumbass!" He was covered with her ashes — his face, his hair, his clothes.

My right palm and crooked ring finger throbbed. For a dizzy, dangerous moment I had the nearly overpowering urge to punch him in the face. But instead I took several deep breaths and gazed at the skyline. I thought of how my brother had gone through life leaving so much wreckage in his wake — failed marriages, estranged children, smashed cars, bounced checks, broken bones, and split skin in barroom brawls — and how my mother had followed along behind trying to pick up the pieces. I understood that he was grieving, too, although perhaps not in a way I could understand.

You don't know shit, Caleb, I wanted to say. You don't even know who I am. But when I spoke these words came out instead: "Why'd you kill my bunny?"

"Funny? What the hell's funny?" The scar on his cheek looked like a white lightning bolt against his livid skin.

I could feel her ashes on my lips. I put the plastic bag back into the urn and pushed it out the window. I pressed my face against the Plexiglas, trying to follow the urn's path down to the sea. But it was already gone.

She had nourished us with her body and her blood, and now we were all that was left of her in the world. I wanted to tell her not to worry, that I would look after Caleb from now on, but I couldn't quite make that commitment. What I told her was this: *Except for each other, Caleb and I are all alone now, flying above the sea in this rickety plane*. I listened for a message from the other side — all I heard was the whining engine, the wind whistling by the window. I felt as if I were in danger of falling out of the plane somehow, that the flimsy door would fly off and I would plummet to the sea below.

I have to try to talk to my brother, I thought. I knew it would take a whole new language, one we had never used before. I closed my eyes. I could feel the sun on my face. I imagined the light entering my body as I began to speak, hoping the right words would come.